Christmas Flowers

Christmas Flowers

A Draegers of Last Stand, Texas Romance

Sasha Summers

TULE
PUBLISHING

Christmas Flowers
Tule Publishing First Printing, October 2019
Copyright© 2019 Sasha Summers

The Tule Publishing, Inc.

ISBN: 978-1-951190-65-1

Chapter One

"CAN YOU SAY that again?" Charlotte covered her ear with her hand and closed her eyes, as if that would somehow make it easier to hear her phone. Because what she'd heard—what she thought she'd heard—had to be wrong. It had to be.

"They've decided to close the imprint, to streamline the magazine into an editorial for one of our better selling publications." Jason Mahaffey had been her boss for the last five years. He had the ability to put a positive spin on most anything. Right now, she could hear his struggle. "I know it's not good news, Charlotte."

Not good news? She blew out a long, steadying breath— her grip on her phone tightening slightly. "No. Definitely not." *A complete and total shock is more like it.*

"But try not to let this ruin your holidays." He paused. "How long has it been since you've spent time with family? Since you've been home?"

"A while." She chewed the inside of her lip. *Too long.* But she wasn't ready to be distracted yet. "I thought—I *heard* there was a merger in the works." Eyes still shut, she mumbled an apology as someone bumped into her. She was, after all, standing on the sidewalk, in everyone's way, smack-dab in front of Austin intercontinental airport, having a telephone conversation. Not exactly the place to come to a hard stop—or have an emotional meltdown. "That a merger—"

"That was wishful thinking." He sighed. "This was more of a…*takeover* than a merger. The board had made up their mind before the meeting ever got started."

Her eyes popped open, taking in the world around her. Families bustled past, festively wrapped packages poking out of their carry-on bags. Some wore Santa hats, others ugly Christmas sweaters—regardless of the sun shining down from the wide Texas sky. It might be Christmas, but that didn't mean the temp was below sixty or that any fluffy white stuff was in her future. A white Christmas, in the Texas Hill Country, was a rarity. But it was magical, when it happened.

"You okay, Charlotte?" he asked.

"Of course." With any luck, it sounded like she meant it. And really, she was. Surprised—fine, totally blown away and shocked—yes, but okay. At least she was home, and not in some far-flung place on the other side of the world. Here, she could regroup and… "This takeover? Do I want to know what this means for me? My job?" Which was basically code for *Do I still have a job.*

"I'm working on that. I am. Obviously, positions are being cut, but you know I believe in your work—" He kept talking, saying all the right things but without the confidence Jason Mahaffey was known for. He was the man who made things happen, took risks, fought for the underdog. And for the last five years, he'd put his heart and soul into his pet project. The *Independent Adventurer* was an eccentric travel magazine that showcased off-the-grid locations for the backpack-toting, no-frills-required, intrepid explorer type of traveler. The concept wasn't exactly mainstream, but they had a devoted readership. At least, she'd *thought* they had a devoted readership. *Apparently not.*

"I'm meeting with the board of directors next week to go over staff—those that are essential, those that aren't. You fall into the first category. I'll do what I can to keep you on the payroll." Jason's forced tone wasn't the least bit encouraging.

"I appreciate that." She nodded, her gaze sweeping the line of vehicles along the curb. Her line of work didn't include much driving, so Grammy had volunteered to pick her up. Her grandmother had been horrified when Charlotte had offered to use a driving service—immediately worrying over Charlotte being abducted, never to be seen or heard from again. Charlotte hadn't pointed out that she spent a good portion of her job alone, in remote and relatively inaccessible parts of the world, but there was no point. Grammy had a penchant for melodrama that made even the most mundane scenarios colorful. But now, she was thankful her grandmother had put her foot down. Seeing her grandmother's smile would help her feel better. So would her hugs. And her nonstop chatter. And, hopefully, a big plate of Christmas cookies. Grammy knew how to find the silver lining in any situation. *Which is exactly what I need.*

Sadly, there was no sign of Krauss's Blooms Florist lilac-colored delivery van and no smiling, arms-spread-wide Grammy waiting. But...something did catch her eye. Rather—someone.

Macon? She blinked. Once. Twice. He was still there.

No. No, no, no!

He waved, all nonchalant, leaning against the hood of his dark green pickup truck. For a split second, it was as if she'd stepped back in time. With his hat tipped back on his head, blue plaid flannel shirt rolled up to his elbows, faded jeans, and leather boots—he looked, as always, like the quintessential cowboy.

Macon Draeger.

Right there. Looking...the way he did. She swallowed against the very large lump suddenly blocking her throat. The question was why? Why was he here? And where was Grammy, her lilac delivery van, reassuring hugs, and escape?

As it was, there was no avoiding Macon. Nope. He was looking at her. Smiling. Walking her way? It wasn't like she could hide; he'd already seen her. Not that she would hide anyway—that would be ridiculous. He was just...him. And she was...an adult. A professional adult.

"I'll call you as soon as I have more news," Jason was saying. "You try to enjoy your visit with your grandmother."

She nodded. Grammy would start worrying as soon as Charlotte told her. Which meant she couldn't tell Grammy—couldn't jeopardize Grammy's long overdue vacation. Charlotte had promised to run Krauss's Blooms for the ten days Grammy would be touring Europe and that promise would stand.

"Charlotte?" Jason Mahaffey asked.

Right. Phone call, Charlotte. He can't see me. "Yes. I will," she answered, attempting not to stare at Macon... Or fidget and shift from foot to foot. Or be super awkward and look everywhere but at him. Especially now that he was standing right in front of her. Staring down at her, way down.

She swallowed again but that lump didn't budge.

When had he gotten so tall? A lock of dark hair fell forward onto his forehead and he smiled. That smile used to make her heart stop.

But that was a long time ago. A very long time ago.

"Hi." He nodded, hands shoved in his pockets, gaze sweeping over her face.

"Hi," she mumbled, her phone still pressed to her ear. Taller, bigger, less boy, way more man. Honestly, he was a giant. A big, tall, manly giant with an incredible smile. Still Macon—but totally different. "Hi." As if that needed repeating.

"Charlotte?" Jason Mahaffey asked. "One more thing."

Her boss. She was on the phone with her boss. That whole professional adult thing. *Right. Ignoring Macon now.* "One more thing?" A hard, knot in her throat. "This is good news, right? I've reached my quota for bad news."

Macon's brows drew together at her words.

"Don't think about this as good or bad news," Jason said. "Life is about viewpoints, you know that. Choices. Consider this a chance to review your options."

"I understand." She tore her gaze from Macon and stared at the toes of her brown leather boots. "There are no guarantees in life. Find the positives."

"Exactly." Jason cleared his throat. "It wouldn't hurt for you to update your résumé, check out other possibilities. I have an inside contact at *National Traveler*—they're going to be looking for a field journalist the beginning of the year. I could put your name forward, if you'd like. Think about it.

But for now, enjoy your time off. I have other calls to make."
A final sigh.

He hung up before she said good-bye. Now she stood, phone still to her ear, staring at her toes, processing his final words. *When your boss tells you to update your résumé, it can only mean one thing.*

It was a shock. The whole conversation. So was being toe-to-toe with the boy she'd left behind. A boy who she'd last talked to, more like pleaded with, standing on the sidewalk in front of an airport nine Christmases ago... And not just any airport. *This airport...*

Nope. Not going there. She had enough to stress over without adding on ancient, and likely forgotten, history. *Please, please let it be forgotten.* Well, not *all* of it, but the end. Definitely the end.

"Everything okay?" Deeper. His voice was different. But familiar.

Not exactly. She nodded. But he didn't need to know that. *More importantly*— "What are you doing here?" Which, considering the amount of irritation in her voice, wasn't exactly the best conversation opener.

He heard it—there was no way to miss it—and tensed. "Edda Mae had a last-minute order." He was reaching for her bag. "I had some errands to run, so I offered to pick you up. Save her the trip."

"You did?" Meaning her grammy, Edda Mae, wasn't coming. So, *he* was her ride? To Last Stand? A small town a good forty-five minutes away. That was if traffic cooperated. *Could this day get more awkward?* Still, it was kind of him to help out Grammy. "You didn't have to do that."

"I know." He smiled, his features relaxing. "But, if you've got everything, we should head out." He glanced at her wheeled suitcase.

"This is everything."

"One?" A dark brow arched.

"When you live out of your suitcase, you learn what's essential and what's not." She shrugged.

"Makes sense." He nodded. "Then let's hit the road. With any luck, we'll miss rush hour." He tugged her suitcase along behind him, heading for the large four-door truck parked along the curb.

"Is that Fern?" The little dog sat inside, ears cocked up, tail wagging a mile a minute. With its mismatched colored patches and shaggy fur, there was no mistaking Grammy's canine companion. "Hiya, Fern. Good to see you, girl."

The little dog cocked its head to one side and barked.

"Happy to see me, too?" She laughed.

"I brought her along. It keeps her out of Edda Mae's hair for a bit." Macon put her suitcase in the back seat, next to Fern. "Fern loves car rides, running back and forth and wearing herself out."

"She's always been a curious little thing. She and Grammy are two peas in a pod." That's the way Grammy put it. Charlotte couldn't agree more.

His blue eyes bounced from her to the dog before he closed the rear door of the truck. Then he held the passenger door open for her. "Need a hand?"

"Nope." She awkwardly climbed up and into the truck cab. It was a higher step than she'd anticipated. There was leg stretching, awkward leaning, and pulling before she

7

managed to get herself up and in—tightly gripping the leather seat back. She wasn't graceful, but she did it. "I'm good."

Macon looked like he was trying not to laugh. "I can see that." He shut the door and walked around the truck.

Fern rested her paws on the seat back so Charlotte reached up, rubbing the little dog behind the ear. "It wasn't that funny, was it?"

Fern's answer was a doggy kiss on her hand.

"I'll take that as a no." When she and Grammy had gone to the shelter looking for the perfect canine companion, it wasn't just the dog's adorable patchwork appearance that caught their attention. It was how Fern had nosed her way around the room to them. When the little dog sat down in front of them, all perked-up ears and wagging tail, it was clear *she* was picking *them*. And, from the look on Grammy's face, it was clear her grandmother was smitten with Fern, as well.

Which was a huge relief for Charlotte.

As much as her grammy argued about not being lonely, Charlotte worried. Bringing Fern home had changed that. Grammy and Fern were the same—full of energy, with a touch of mischief. Imagining Grammy being followed around by the attentive pup, who thought her grandmother hung the moon, instantly brought a smile to Charlotte's face. And eased any lingering guilt she had for her infrequent visits the last few years.

Macon climbed into the driver's seat, buckled up, and turned on the ignition. "You two ready?"

Fern barked and sat on the seat.

Charlotte had no choice but to laugh. She reached out, rubbing behind one of the dog's tan ears again. "I think that was a yes?"

Fern made a whimper-bark and covered Charlotte's hand with wet doggy kisses.

"Looks like she remembers you." Macon pulled his massive vehicle away from the curb and into the traffic.

"I'd be heartbroken if she didn't. I was sort of the one who brought her and Grammy together." With a final scratch, Charlotte turned and stared out the front windshield.

"Wouldn't worry too much about that. You tend to leave an impression." The words were soft. And neutral. But she couldn't help but think there was a hidden meaning there, if she chose to look for one.

She didn't.

"How's life, Macon?" It wasn't as generic as asking about the weather, but it was a start. "Your family?" Then she paused, remembering. "I'm so sorry about your father. Really—"

"Your flowers meant the world to us—to my mom." His blue eyes were warm. "Especially since you were, where? Thailand?"

How did he know? Her article on the work the Huai Kha Khaeng Wildlife Sanctuary was doing to protect tigers and their habitat hadn't been printed yet. Which meant... "Grammy oversharing again?"

"She's proud of you." He chuckled.

He was driving, so he probably didn't realize that she was studying him. But she was. And she needed to stop. "It helps

9

SASHA SUMMERS

that I'm her *only* grandchild." She toyed with the strap on her purse. "Probably a good thing, too, or you'd be forced to listen to boring stories about all of her grandkids."

"Not boring." He shook his head. "Not to hear Edda Mae tell them, anyway. You know your grandmother."

Grammy and her storytelling. She should have been an actress. "I do." She smiled at him, her eyes tangling up with his until she forced her attention out the window.

"If she's not telling stories, she's sharing her opinions—like it or not." But there was a smile in his voice.

She almost looked at him. Almost. "I'm sure she has all sorts of opinions about me."

He nodded, more chuckles. "Heaps of them."

"Really?" It was a joke. Sort of. Her grammy, Edda Mae to the rest of the world, was the one person she could always count on. Her grammy's opinion mattered to her. A lot. She was close to her parents, but their missionary work took them to remote places all over the world, oftentimes without the ability to call or Skype or email. With her likewise mobile lifestyle, the chance of getting a letter that wasn't already weeks behind was slim. But Grammy? Well, she was always a phone call away—anytime, day or night. "Should I be worried?"

"Nope." Macon glanced at her.

It was impossible to miss just how kind the years had been to him. He'd always been cute—the sort of cute that made her blush whenever their eyes had met. Now…he was a different level of cute. Handsome. *Very handsome.* The threat of a full-on blushing episode was all too real. *No, no, no.* "Your brothers all good?" she asked—actually, squeaked

10

was more like it—as she fumbled with her large leather purse, looking for her phone. She wasn't necessarily trying to avoid staring at Macon. Okay, maybe she was. Why was her purse so big anyway?

He filled her in on his family and their ranch. "Kolton is still Kolton—but he's my brother so I put up with him." He grinned. "My older brother Lam is married now. He has twin girls. They're the cutest things—always running around in sparkly wings, looking for fairies." He paused. "They haven't figured out the difference between fireflies and fairies yet."

The image his words painted had Charlotte pausing mid phone search. "That's wonderful. Childhood can be such a special time." Hers had been all over the place—unless she'd been with her grammy.

Now that her purse was in her lap, it was impossible to ignore the vibrating coming from inside. But, after her talk with Jason Mahaffey, she figured the calls were likely from other coworkers, who were sounding off about their beloved magazine being devoured by a larger, more commercial, more lucrative publication. She was the one who had been with *Independent Adventurer* the longest, so they must think she'd have the inside scoop—she always had. But this time...this time she was just as in the dark as the rest of them. Equally adrift and frustrated by this unexpected turn. After upending her purse's contents into her lap, she located her phone.

With a muffled groan, she scrolled through the frantic messages and handful of voice mails she'd have to listen to.

"You sure everything is okay?" Macon asked, concern in

his voice.

She nodded but didn't look at him. If she looked at him, in all his blush-inducing handsomeness, she might pour out her worries on his big, capable shoulders—like she had so many times in the past. In an attempt to give Charlotte a *normal* high school experience, she'd lived with Grammy in Last Stand while she went to high school. Those four years created some of her most treasured memories. Many of them—most, really—included Macon. He had known her better than anyone. Spending hours talking about their hopes, dreams, and fears had led to a strong connection. *The strongest.* He'd understood the way her mind worked, and stuck around anyway. Nothing was off-limits between them. It would be so easy to tell him about work. Money. Future prospects. As well as the growing realization, taking root long before the buy-out-merger news, that she was ready for a change. He'd listen to all of it because he'd always been the best listener. With the best shoulders. And now those shoulders were way broader...

He had been the best listener. Had been. In the past. Years ago.

Not now. Now, they weren't confidants, best friends...and so much more.

Now they were different people. He was a manly, handsome, giant cowboy with a devastating smile. She was a world-traveling photojournalist with a penchant for exotic flowers and teas. What could they possibly have in common now?

Edda Mae, maybe.

Beyond that?

Nothing.

And that was fine. She was here for a reason. Grammy was finally taking her dream cruise through Europe—while Charlotte ran Krauss's Blooms. Grammy would be home in time for the Christmas Ball and Charlotte would leave the day after Christmas. That was the plan. That *had* been the plan. Now, with work, the plan might change a bit. But whatever happened, those changes would have nothing to do with Macon Draeger.

MACON HAD BEEN accused of many things in his life. Being quiet wasn't one of them. He was the sibling who irritated the rest with his teasing and jokes. Conversation was second nature to him. If there was an uncomfortable silence, he could always fill it.

Always.

Until now.

Because Charlotte Krauss was sitting next to him and he was an idiot.

His hands flexed on the leather-padded steering wheel. It had been nine years since he'd last seen her. Nine. Sure, Edda Mae shoved postcards and pictures in his face whenever he stopped by her flower shop, but that wasn't the same thing as this. Sharing space. Air.

Air so loaded with something, the weight of it strained his shoulders.

But she wasn't talking and he couldn't push her. She also wasn't looking at him much—which bothered him. Was she that upset to see him? Maybe so. The last time she'd visited, she'd made time for lunch with his sister Tabby and a visit with his mother, but not with him. She hadn't even given him so much as a quick hello. While it shouldn't matter, it did.

"Edda Mae said you were in Thailand for the tigers?" Maybe he could draw her out over tigers—they were her favorite.

Her gray eyes locked with his. "They were incredible, Macon." An almost dream-like smile settled on her lips. "I cried, I admit it. I guess, seeing them out in the open—wild and free—just seemed...I don't know, right. And humbling. And, honestly, slightly terrifying. They are beautiful, but they were massive and dangerous. Real predators. It was just *incredible*."

Macon tore his gaze from hers and guided his truck back into their lane. He needed to pay less attention on Charlotte, and more on the road. He sighed. She'd always done that. Distracted him—without even trying.

"When does the article come out?" He'd avoided her first few articles—reading her words was too much like having a conversation with her. He'd been too overwhelmed putting his heart and his world back together to consider 'hearing' her in his head. Not then.

But Edda Mae was a proud grandma. Whether he liked it or not, Edda Mae made sure to get a print copy of those editions, just for him. When the hurt of what could have been finally gave way to the way things were, he'd read most of her work. It was no surprise that he enjoyed her writing— enjoyed the brief vacation from his day-in and day-out work to some remote corner of the world. Through her words, he absorbed the scents of the air, the local flavors, and the incredible beauty she always managed to find with her lens. This one, about something she loved so dearly, would likely be her best work yet.

"I'm not sure." She was staring at her phone again, her nails fiddling with its silicone case. "But I'm sure Grammy will let you know when it does."

Her phone pinged and she turned it over, her nose wrinkling as her gaze fixed on the screen.

"Glad to have a break?" he asked.

She nodded, turning the phone over and staring out the front windshield. But he saw the way she wrinkled up her nose and knew what it meant. Charlotte was upset.

"I guess running Edda Mae's shop isn't exactly a break." It's not like driving in silence was a bad thing. But having Charlotte upset was.

"I don't mind." She shrugged. "It's nice to stay put for a while, especially here. And Grammy's shop. You know..." Her gaze darted his way. "I've always loved the shop."

"With its cracking plaster and leaky faucet?" he teased.

"Especially the cracking plaster. Besides, the leaky faucet is an easy fix." Her brows rose as she faced him. "Being at Grammy's is better than sleeping in a tent or trying to wash under a spigot or, maybe it's just me, eating roasted crickets." She was watching him now, most likely trying to gauge his reaction.

"I prefer mine battered and fried." He nodded. "With a side of ranch dressing. Even some cream gravy works."

She laughed. "You joke, but that might have done the

trick."

"Isn't that part of being an independent adventurer, though? What you always wanted? The whole thing—room and board and lack of running water and all that?" He wanted to know. There were times he wondered about the world beyond his small hometown and family ranch, for all its thousands of acres. He might wonder sometimes, but not enough to pack up a tent and leave the people and places he loved behind. To him, the community had always been the cornerstone of his world.

"It is." She paused. "*But* it's my job to make it look nice and shiny. Sometimes, that takes a *lot* of work."

"You'd never know it." And just like that, he saw himself the way she did. "And to clear things up, I'm not some creeper trying to keep up with you through your magazine articles. Edda Mae—"

"Oh, I can imagine. How many copies does she buy? Knowing her, she probably gives them out with flower arrangements." She was laughing again.

"I will neither confirm nor deny that." He leaned closer. "But she has and she does." Her scent tickled his nose. Apples. Her favorite scent. Even after he sat back in his seat, the odor lingered, making it hard to keep his eyes on the road.

Charlotte was beautiful. She always had been, with long, dark, thick hair she often ended up twisting up or clipping back. And big, gray eyes that looked close enough to see beyond the surface. She was barely over five feet, but she was too feisty to be considered short or small. Her smile lit up a room and her laugh was contagious. In the past, he'd spent hours doing things to make her laugh, just because he loved the sound of it.

"Last Stand still does Christmas in a big way, doesn't it?" She'd turned in her seat, more at ease now. "An extra-large serving of holiday spirit?"

"For a small town, there's nothing small about the way we celebrate Christmas." He nodded. "It's not exactly exotic, I know, but I'd say the holidays are impressive nonetheless."

"Good. I love everything about Christmas here." Her lips quirked. "I'm trying to remember the last time I had a tree."

He stared at her. "You? Without a tree?" One thing about Charlotte: she was part Christmas elf—or so she'd always said. He remembered her enthusiasm all too well. The day after Thanksgiving, the Christmas boxes were unearthed and Edda Mae's cozy home had been transformed into a cozy Christmas cottage. "I'm having a hard time picturing that."

"Believe it or not, this is only my sixth Christmas here, Macon." Her brows arched high again, for emphasis.

"Really? Huh?" He paused. The Christmases they'd spent together were some of his favorite memories. And some of the worst. "Is that right?"

She nodded. "There were the four during high school, when I lived with Grammy, and..." her gaze fell and her posture stiffened "...then, when I came back that...first Christmas—in college."

That Christmas. It was something else he remembered all too well. Every last kick-to-the-gut detail. He'd hoped, with time, the memories would fade. They hadn't.

"How are your folks?" he asked, pushing the conversation forward. Charlotte's parents, like Charlotte, never stayed in one place too long.

"Last I heard from them, they were doing well." She shook her head, a heavy curl falling free from the knot at the base of her head. "They've been working in Serbia for a couple of years now. They've mentioned retirement but I can't imagine them actually doing anything about it. They're both so...so active."

"When they do retire, they'll have more than earned it." Maybe then, they'd spend more time together as a family. He knew Edda Mae missed her son and daughter-in-law. And Charlotte? Edda Mae had been both a parent and a grandmother to Charlotte. When she'd moved here for high school, it had been Edda Mae who went to all of her art exhibitions and award ceremonies, threw birthday and holiday parties, and sat in the front row at her graduation.

There were times when his family was a little too in each other's business but he couldn't imagine going one week, let alone months or years, without seeing them. His brother, Sam, had put himself in a sort of self-imposed exile—refusing letters or visits from the rest of the family. Macon missed him. But he hadn't given up on him, and neither had his siblings.

"Who did Lam marry?" she asked. "Is it someone I'd know?"

He frowned. "I'm not sure. She might have been here one of the summers you visited. Do you remember Gwen Hobbs? Gwen Draeger now."

She leaned her elbow on the door rest and tapped her chin with her pointer finger. "The name is familiar. But it might have been from Tabby's emails?"

"They haven't been married all that long. They're still in that doe-eyed honeymoon phase that can get downright awkward." He didn't mind it too much. Seeing his brother happy after so long gave him hope he'd have the same thing someday, too.

Maybe. Maybe not. It was sort of a relief that there was no one around who tempted him to risk his heart. There hadn't been in years—not since Charlotte Krauss had left.

Chapter Two

CHARLOTTE STOOD ON the brick street, staring at her grandmother's beloved florist shop. The large picture window that opened onto Main Street was a veritable Christmas-scape. Green garland, red poinsettia, sheets of cotton batting sprinkled with glitter, and a wreath glistening with silver balls and small bells invited passers-by to peek inside. From where she stood, she could almost smell the cinnamon wicker brooms or braided candy canes her grandmother sold this time of year. Cinnamon was one of her favorite scents. Cinnamon and ginger—especially when they were mixed together and baked up in some of Grammy's gingerbread cookies.

Grammy loved Christmas with every fiber of her being. It was something she'd passed on to Charlotte. This year, for the first time in far too long, Charlotte was spending Christmas here. And she was going to enjoy every single second of it. Starting now. Whatever happened with her job could wait until the holidays were over. Until then, she was going to throw herself, one hundred and ten percent, into this holiday season.

"You lost?" Macon asked. "I know it's been a while, and all, but nothing ever changes here."

Which was comforting to hear. And yet, staring up at the

too-tall, too-handsome, too…Macon, she wondered if that was true. The town might not change but the people definitely had. He was proof of that. She hadn't had to crane her neck quite so far nine years ago. Now? She was looking up, way up, to meet his gaze.

What else had changed about him?

"Glad to be home?" he asked, his smile growing.

Fine. His smile hadn't changed. At all. It used to warm her up from the inside. *Used to.* She'd missed his smile, ached for the sound of his voice, for months after that horrible day. Giving him up had been one of the hardest decisions she'd ever made. But it had been the right thing, for both of them. It wouldn't have been fair to hold on to his heart while she was traipsing around the world. Especially since she hadn't known when, or if, she'd be ready to settle in one place. If he'd found someone else… She swallowed. Well, he'd deserved happiness. She didn't want to hold him back.

"Charlotte!" Grammy erupted from the shop with a happy cry, her arms held wide. "Look at you." She held her away long enough to do a quick head-to-toes sweep, then tugged her into a tight hug.

Finally. Being wrapped in her grandmother's arms always had a steadying effect on her. "I'm so happy to be here, Grammy." She closed her eyes, the cares and fears of the morning slipping away, for now at least. *Grammy magic.* If there was a way to bottle the comfort and love in her grandmother's hug, life would be easier.

"You say that now, but you're the one stuck working while I'm sailing off into the sunset." With a pat on her back, Grammy took Charlotte's hand and stepped back. This time, her inspection was a little too close for comfort. "You look plum tuckered out."

She shrugged. No point arguing—she was.

"What do you think, Macon?" Grammy asked. "Isn't it good to have our girl back in Last Stand?"

'Our girl'? Really Grammy? Years ago, sure. Still, it was a reminder. Grammy wouldn't be the only one to bring up their past, give a pointed dig or two, or generally make things as uncomfortable as possible when the two of them were together. That was why she'd avoided him her last visit. Clearly, that wasn't going to be an option this time around. The best she could do? Avoid heartburn. To do that, she'd need to take the teasing and comments and side-eyed looks and whispers in stride and not let them bother her. Or Macon—bother her, that is. Starting now. She met his brilliant blue gaze, her voice only slightly high and pinched as she said, "It's good to be back."

His gaze held hers, intense and totally unreadable. "I'm sure you have a lot of catching up to do," Macon said, a smile in his voice.

Fern barked and ran around his legs before trotting to the front door of the shop to sit and wait.

Grammy tugged on her arm. "You betcha, we do. And I still have to pack before I hightail it out of here tomorrow."

"You haven't packed?" Charlotte shook her head. "You do like to live on the edge, don't you?"

"Sounds like a busy night." Macon chuckled, pulling his keys from his pocket. "If you need anything, help with the shop or something, give me a call."

Charlotte looked his way. Way up. Seriously, the man was a giant. "I've got it covered." Did she sound snippy? She didn't mean to sound snippy. She didn't mean to stare or blush or feel so incredibly awkward—but she did that, too.

His blue eyes were steady on her face. "It is good to see you, Charlotte."

It was good to see him, too. Weird. Unsettling. But...good. "Thank you for the ride." This time, there was no snippiness involved.

"You'll be seeing her tomorrow, don't forget." Grammy waved him off. "I'll have that wreath you ordered for your mother ready. Can you pick it up on your lunch hour?"

Tomorrow? She'd see him tomorrow. Great. But after that, surely, they wouldn't be running into each other. Yes, it was a small town but this was a flower shop. And the only reason for Macon Draeger to frequent a flower shop was for flowers. Unless he had a special someone he hadn't mentioned, there was no reason he'd be a frequent customer.

The whole special someone question stuck in the center of her chest. Sticky and heavy and too uncomfortable to ignore. She tried, she really did, but the smile she'd pinned in place wavered.

What is wrong with me? Just overtired. And really stressed. *Nothing more.* If Macon Draeger had someone special in his life, that would be just fine by her. Great, really.

"Sounds good." He touched the brim of his hat. "Guess I'll see you tomorrow, then." The smile he turned on her grandmother was pretty awe-inspiring. "You have a wonderful time on your trip, Edda Mae. I expect a PowerPoint presentation when you get back."

"Don't you worry." Her grandmother reached up to pat his cheek. "Now that I know how to add music and such, it'll be like a movie."

Her grammy was a firm believer in learning new things. Her latest self-educational focus had been online tech training for social media. Not that Grammy had any social media accounts. Still, her grandmother believed in being prepared.

"I'll bring some popcorn." Macon gave Grammy a hug, nodded her way, and set off down the street.

Charlotte refused to watch him go, although she did sneak a glance back—long enough to see him look back over his shoulder at her. She did not blush and almost trip over her grandmother in her haste to get inside the flower shop. Fine, she did. And it was embarrassing.

Grammy was shaking her head as she closed the shop door behind them. "Still skittish around that boy."

"I am not." The words were out in a rush, earning a knowing glance from Grammy. *Awesome. Way to play it cool.* She tried again. "Besides, he's over six feet and has way too much facial hair to be called a boy." She tugged her wheeled suitcase behind her. Fern circled her bag, sniffing it in rapid helicopter-like sniffs.

"You noticed that, did you?" Her grandmother's bright eyes were alight with mischief.

"Do you hear her, Fern?" Charlotte knelt to offer the dog a pat. "The last thing we want to do is talk about Macon Draeger, isn't that right, Fern? I want to hear all about you. The shop. Your quilting club—"

"Fine, fine." Grammy turned the 'open' sign to 'closed' and locked the door. "Let's get home and get you settled, first, though. Okay? It's close enough to five to close up, anyhow."

Fern trotted after her grandmother, giving Charlotte a chance to stare around the shop. So many of her favorite memories happened right here. Maybe that was why she adored the place so much. Every inch of it. From its exposed brick to the pieces of painted broken plaster still haphazardly covering the wall here and there. A floral wall tapestry hung in the middle, covered with postcards, pictures, and whatever odds and ends Grammy chose. The opposite wall was covered by a massive cooler that hummed and clicked. Inside, vibrant buds of color, pops of texture, and bold shades of green were on display. If she cracked the door, just an inch, she had no doubt her senses would be overcome with the glorious scents inside. "It's just the same."

Grammy nodded, the creases of her forehead deepening.

"That's a good thing." Charlotte stood. "What's wrong?"

Just like that, her grandmother was smiling again. "Not a thing." Her gray-blue eyes were doing yet another inspection. "You're too skinny."

"No. I'm not." Then she stopped. "But I wouldn't say no to a gingerbread man, or two, if you happened to have some sitting around."

"Sitting around, huh?" Grammy giggled, reaching for her hand. "Come on. I have a few pans just waiting for decorations. Some with raisins, some with red hots—"

"Some with both?"

Grammy nodded. "Of course."

Which made happiness bubble up inside her.

Grammy turned off lights, checked the cooler temperature, then grabbed her massive satchel. "You ready?" she asked Fern, clipping the Monet water-lily printed leash onto the dog's collar. "Me, too."

The walk from Krauss's Blooms to Grammy's little cottage took less than ten minutes. It wouldn't have taken even three minutes if they hadn't bumped into Dotty Allen, who ran one of the hair salons, Jerry and Ida Heinesman taking their evening stroll, as well as dealing with Fern's preoccupation with every squirrel along the way. Charlotte hadn't realized just how many squirrels called Last Stand home—until now.

When they rounded the corner, the sight of Grammy's tiny pink cottage, with its white wicker porch furniture and painted latticework, was a welcome site. She reached for the gate latch but the hinge was stubborn and took more force than she remembered. When it finally creaked open, the noise made her wince.

"I know." Grammy glanced at the gate. "It's on my list."

"List?" Charlotte echoed.

"I've got a honey-do list a mile long...but no honey to do it." She winked. "Not that there aren't a few suitors."

That brought her up short. Grammy was dating? *This* was great news. "Do tell."

While Charlotte followed her grandmother down the small hall to the guest bedroom, she got an earful about the three men doing an admirable job of wooing her grammy. While she was unpacking everything she owned in the world into the dresser and closet, Grammy kept right on chattering.

By the time she'd finished up, it was obvious to Charlotte that Grammy had a favorite. From the smile on her face and the tone of her voice, her grandmother exhibited all the signs of having a crush.

When Grammy added, "Lewis was a master gardener," Charlotte knew the other two didn't stand a chance. For Grammy, having a green thumb was a must-have. The memories she had of her grandfather were hazy around the edges but one thing she knew: they'd shared a deep love of gardening and green, growing things. They'd spent hours planting and weeding their bloom-heavy flower beds and potted plants. One of Charlotte's all-time favorite pictures was of the three of them—Granddad, Grammy, and a five-year-old Charlotte with muddy knees and a mile-wide grin.

"Lewis, hm?" she asked.

Grammy waved a dismissive hand. *Wait. Grammy is blushing?* She was. Her outspoken, unflappable, absolutely adorable grammy was blushing? Maybe she'd run the shop *and* get to know this Lewis Master Gardener guy—just to make sure he had honorable intentions toward her grammy, of course.

Fern leapt up on her bed, resting her chin on her little paws to stare up at her with big doe eyes.

"That's her hungry face." Grammy laughed. "She turns on the charm when she wants something."

"Well, she's asking so nicely, how can I say no?" Charlotte sat on the bedside, rubbing the little dog behind the ear. "We're going to get along just fine, aren't we, Fern?"

Fern sat up, tail wagging as she climbed into Charlotte's lap.

"Just don't let her eat too much." Grammy shook her head. "She's cute and she knows it so she'll try to get extra treats."

"Speaking of treats." Charlotte stood, her stomach grumbling.

"That's all you have?" Grammy eyed the empty bag.

She nodded. "That's it."

"I'll make some hot chocolate to have with our cookies and you can tell me all about your latest globe-trotting adventures." Grammy paused, hugging her again. "I'm so glad you're here, Charlotte. I know I have no right to ask, but, if you can, I'd love for you to stay a while longer after I get back? Maybe spend New Year's here, with me? It would be the best way to start the New Year."

Charlotte kept right on hugging her grandmother. Stay here, through the holidays, with Grammy and Fern? Why not? It's not like she had any place to go. Now that work was up in the air, her future was wide open. The thought of staying here longer was tempting. And being wrapped up in Grammy's steady arms felt like exactly the right place to be.

MACON TOOK THE wrench from his brother, then handed it back. "The adjustable. Not the combo."

Kolton swapped out the wrenches. "How does she look?" He nudged Macon with the toe of his boot.

Macon stared at the pipe, wrench in hand, considering his answer. How did Charlotte look? If he used the wrong word, wore the wrong expression, Kolton would read an encyclopedia of information into it. Better to keep it simple. Charlotte looked... "Good." He tightened the outer seal on the pipe. "Turn on the faucet. Slowly."

Kolton did, both faucets, full stream.

Macon winced, waiting for the pipe to spew water all over him.

"Looks like you fixed it," Kolton said, kneeling down beside him. "I'm sort of bummed. I was hoping you'd end up soaked."

Macon glared at his brother. "Thanks for all the help."

"You're the 'Macon-it-better' guy. Not me." Kolton handed him a towel.

He stood, wiping his hands and glaring at his brother. The wince-worthy catchphrase was linked to the home repair business he'd been running for the last five years. MD Repairs was the official name. The 'Macon-it-better' thing was courtesy of one of his clients. Which one, he had no idea. But it had stuck and spread. A catchphrase nightmare.

"Does this mean you're not going to answer the question? About Charlotte, I mean. Good? That's it? Good as in, good?" Kolton winked, the tone in his voice erasing any misunderstanding as he added, "Or good as in *good*?" He bobbed his eyebrows for emphasis.

"Kolt." Macon shook his head. Kolton lived for this— teasing and poking and making him squirm. Macon usually found him funny, when he wasn't on the receiving end of the joke. "Why does it matter? She's...Charlotte, okay? What else do you want me to say?"

"Whoa, didn't mean to 'Macon-you-crazy.'" Kolton laughed, then leaned away from Macon's scowl. "I'm kidding, man. Kidding. It's my job, as your brother. Besides, no way would I go after your high school sweetheart. I get it. First love, and all that. It's like a life-bond thing. The whole world knows it." But Kolton was grinning, pleased with himself, when he was done.

"Did you say life bond?" Macon wiped the grease from his hand. "If you're done trying to get a rise out of me, how about we talk about something else?"

"Sure." Kolton pulled himself onto the kitchen counter. "Did you hear Wichita Falls is looking for a new fire chief?"

From one sensitive topic to another. Macon started packing up his tools.

When he didn't respond, Kolton added, "I thought so." He crossed his arms over his chest. "Did Diego call you? Diego Rivera? From the Wichita Falls city council?"

Macon leaned against the counter, across from his brother. "I talked to him." Diego Rivera had been pretty persuasive. Basically, if Macon joined the Wichita Falls team, he'd be doing the same thing he'd been doing as acting fire marshal here in Last Stand for the last three years, but on a bigger scale. Between the pay and the benefits and the resources, it was one of those irresistible opportunities... Only it was in Wichita Falls.

"Are you going to apply for the job?" Kolton lowered his voice as Old John, one of the foremen at Draeger Ranch, walked into the bunkhouse kitchen.

"You fix it?" John asked, opening the refrigerator and pulling out a pitcher of iced tea. "All night long, I hear it. Drip-drip-drip."

Macon nodded. "It just needed a new seal. Should be

good to go." For now. It wouldn't hurt to look into new pipes and replace the wheezing refrigerator. He'd talk to Lam about it. His big brother was all about keeping their foremen happy.

John poured himself a tall glass of tea, put the pitcher back, and leveled a steady look Macon's way. "Guess we'll see." He left the kitchen, tea in hand.

"If I ever get that crotchety in my old age, smack me on the back of the head." Kolton stared after the older man.

"Oh, yeah, smacking you on the back of the head is bound to put you in a better frame of mind." Macon sighed. "This is his home. It'd irritate me if I heard dripping water all night."

"He's been like that for the last eight or nine years, Macon. I'm pretty sure it has nothing to do with the faucet."

No arguing that. Old John had been there as long as Macon could remember and he'd never been someone you could describe as pleasant. But the man was good at his job. He worked hard, and was reliable—which made him the gold standard of foremen. And, crotchety or not, the old man was family.

"I'm hungry. You hungry?"

Kolton shrugged. "I'm not sure I can stomach another meal with Lam and Gwen being all moony-eyed."

"Think of the kids, Kolt." Macon threw an arm around his brother's shoulders. "Poor Amy and Jilly. The girls will have to suffer through all the 'sugars' and 'honeys' without us around to cut through all the lovey-dovey hooey."

Kolton eyes widened. "Low blow, man. Low blow, using the kids like that."

"I'm just too hungry to drive into town to eat." Which was partly true. The other part? He had to take a shower and get cleaned up before he headed into town to pick up his mother's Christmas wreath from Krauss's Blooms—preferably without Kolton riding along.

"Fine," Kolton grumbled.

Gwen and her mother were sharing kitchen duties, meaning the food at the ranch was always incredible and they were all in danger of needing larger pants. Not that any of them were complaining. There was nothing like home-made scones or freshly baked bread for their toast, topped with preserves made from the Draeger peach orchard. Or salad harvested from the garden, with perfectly seasoned grilled chicken. Classics like crisp and flaky chicken fried steak, as well as tender and juicy pot roast. And, of course, dessert every night.

Today's lunch was club sandwiches, home-fried sweet potato chips, and a fresh green salad. While they were munching, his mind drifted to Charlotte's comment the other day about having to eat bugs. He'd figured she'd been dining on exotic fare all over the world. But there was exotic, and then there was *exotic*. Was having a full kitchen and a grocery store close by a good thing? Or was she missing her vagabond existence?

"I thought I'd go into town and see Charlotte," Tabby, his sister, announced. "Girls' night. Dinner. That sort of thing."

Which meant Tabby could pick up the wreath.

"Is Charlotte the one you were telling me about?" Gwen asked, her lightning-quick glance his way assuring him that *everyone* in the house was familiar with his first love—and his first heartbreak.

Maybe it was better if he didn't go into town. He didn't want people, especially the people under this roof, reading things into his actions.

"She is awesome, Gwen. You'll love her. She's creative and funny and just…cool. Her folks go all over the world, working for a water-for-everyone charity. When she wasn't traveling the world with them, she'd stay with Edda Mae. And her stories? Fascinating." She wagged her carrot stick at Gwen. "Now she's traveling the world solo. She is that kind of fearless."

"Is she as intimidating as she sounds?" Gwen asked, wiping her daughter Jilly's cheek and offering her other daughter, Amy, a napkin.

No. If there was one word that did not describe Charlotte, it was intimidating.

"Not at all." Tabby shook her head. "Not the last time I saw her anyway. It has been a few years."

"I'd really like to meet her." Gwen nodded.

"She's here through Christmas, so we will definitely have to get together, at least once, the three of us." Tabby's borderline sympathetic smile had him rolling his eyes.

Why did everyone think he was carrying a torch for Charlotte? It's not like he'd been living like a monk. He'd dated. Went out. Did what he wanted, when he wanted.

Tabby should definitely be the one to pick up the wreath.

"You're awfully quiet," Lam, the eldest, said. "Something on your mind?"

Macon's mind scrambled, hoping—praying—he could come up with an answer that they'd all believe and move on.

"The decorating committee for the Christmas Ball," he grumbled.

A wave of sympathetic 'ohs' rolled around the table.

"How did you get roped into that?" Gwen asked.

"It's another fire marshal thing," Kolton filled in. "One of the perks."

"And he's Macon," Tabby added. "Everyone loves our brother. He's patient and fair, and goes above and beyond to help out."

"You mean, he's a pushover," Kolton added, laughing.

Macon breathed a sigh of relief. He didn't mind being on the committee for this year's Christmas Ball decorating committee so much, because it might be his last here in Last Stand. The job in Wichita Falls was full-time, which meant a move several hours from here. There'd be no more part-time repair work or calls at weird hours over lightbulbs that needed replacing or 'strange noises' from someone's water heater. It also meant round-the-clock responsibility for a full-scale firehouse. He'd been licensed and certified through his training for the National Guard—as well as their leadership program. This job would give him the chance to use that training and give him his own backyard. But was that what he really wanted? It had been a long time since he'd thought about that.

What did he want?

Most days, he was busy from sunup to sundown, doing what needed to be done. He loved his family home. Riding out at dawn and watching the sun rise over the hills filled him with peace and kept him grounded. There was something rewarding about working the same land that had been in his family for generations. When he wasn't here, he was at the firehouse. His father had been proud of him for that— for his National Guard service and his position as city fire marshal. As if that wasn't enough, he had his business. For him, taking care of the people in his life—earning and keeping the respect of those he admired—was important.

But Last Stand wasn't the only community where he could make a difference. Maybe a move, a fresh start, would open new doors and further opportunities to him.

If that's what he wanted. He only wished he knew.

Chapter Three

CHARLOTTE STOOD ON the top step of the collapsible stool. She grasped a strand of white twinkle lights in the tips of her fingers and stretched as far as her five-foot-one inches would allow.

Fern barked.

"I'm being careful." She was so close. The hook was right there. So, so, close.

Then the little bell over the door rang. Suddenly, she lost her precarious balance, and felt herself slipping. One minute, she was on the stool, and the next, she was falling, the stained concrete floor rising up to meet her.

Until she wasn't. She'd been caught.

Cradled.

Against Macon Draeger's wall of a chest.

One look told her he wasn't any happier about her risky near-contortionist maneuverings to hang the lights than Fern had been. But Fern was still wagging her tail and looking at her with adoration. Macon was not.

The way his gaze bounced from the stool, to the hook, to her, she knew exactly what he was thinking. His jaw muscle tightened and his hands pressed her closer against him. Not that she was thinking about the wall of muscle beneath his shirt. Or the sturdy strength of Macon's arms holding her.

Or how familiar his touch was. Nope. Not at all. She was concentrating on breathing. And thinking that maybe, just maybe, she'd been a teeny-tiny bit careless.

Macon's blue eyes locked with hers. A crease formed between his brows and he looked like he was about to say something. She was in trouble.

A nervous giggle rose up. "Thank you. Would you mind putting me down now?"

"It depends." He had a far more impressive scowl than she remembered. "Will you stay on the ground, or are you going to try *that* again?"

Her gaze darted to the hook, the one she still had to reach in order to hang the string of lights. "Um…"

His gaze followed. With a sigh he said, "If I hang the lights, will you stay on the ground?"

"Yes. Thank you." And just like that, she was standing on the floor—trying not to marvel at just how strong and inflexible Macon's arms and chest had been. He was a human rock. A giant, human rock.

One thing that hadn't changed about Macon? His warmth. She hadn't felt the slightest chill, until he'd set her down. A slight shiver ran along her skin.

"You realize you could have hurt yourself?" He moved the stool a few inches closer, climbed up the steps and successfully snagged the light cord on the hook before he'd finished the question.

"It took you, what, five seconds, tops? I've been trying to do for the last fifteen minutes." She frowned at him. "Well, that's not right."

He frowned back. "That I'm taller than you, or that you

were willing to hurt yourself for a strand of lights?"

It was kind of hard not to see his point when he put it that way. "You're not just taller than *me*. You're taller than...*everyone*."

His expression eased. "That might be an exaggeration."

"No. It's not." She shook her head. "You are a giant." *Was that a smile?* It looked like he was trying not to smile.

His gaze fell from hers and he folded up the stool. "Where does this go?" He paused. "Or should I take it with me, just in case?"

"Those are the only lights I have." *For now.*

His scowl was back. "That's not exactly comforting, Charlotte."

Something about the way he said 'Charlotte' captured her full attention. Part scold, part plea. That his scowl gave way to something earnest—concerned—only added to the odd tug hearing him say her name caused. "You don't have to take my stepstool."

"Still not comforting." He ran a hand over his face.

"Grammy said I could make a few changes." Changes that would likely require more time on the stepstool—not that he needed to know that.

"What sort of changes are we talking about?" He had his brows raised, his hands on his hips, his no-nonsense posture on high. "You realize this is a historical structure? Special wiring. Special plumbing. Changes require permits."

"Permits?" She stepped closer, reaching for the stepstool. "I'm not knocking down walls or anything. I'm just stringing some lights...and stuff."

He held the stool away. "Again, you're not doing much

to win your case here."

"As far as I know, I do not need to win my case to do what I want, *Mr.* Draeger. It's my grandmother's store." She did her best to exude calm. "While I appreciate your concern, I am perfectly capable of taking care of things here. I have your Christmas wreath ready. If you'll allow me to put my grammy's stool away, I'll get it for you."

He was staring at her, long and hard, as if she was a puzzle he couldn't quite fit together. With a resigned sigh, he handed over the stepstool.

"Thank you." She carried it to the back of the shop, stowing it under a worktable—and out of sight—in case he changed his mind. Fern trotted behind her, climbing into her doggy bed and curling into a ball. Charlotte smiled, then found the wreath she and Grammy had finished last night and carried it out.

"How's day one going?" he asked, taking the wreath.

"Fairly uneventful." She shrugged. "I have a novel of a note I'm supposed to read when I get home tonight but, unless Grammy has some surprise planned, I'm expecting it to stay that way."

"Novel, huh?" He shook his head. "I wouldn't put off reading it. Edda Mae is a big fan of surprises."

She glanced up at him. "You think so?" Grammy and her penchant for drama. It would be like her to slip something in under the radar, just to keep Charlotte on her toes.

"I know so." He chuckled. "If I were you, I'd be worried."

Seconds later, she had her purse on the counter and was pulling the lilac-colored folder with the Krauss's Blooms logo out. "How bad could it be?" She opened the envelope and scanned her grandmother's flowery script. A few sections were tabbed. "Delivery dates… What to do if the cooler freezes up…" She kept reading. "Her garden…" Which reminded her of Lewis, the bachelor master gardener. "What can you tell me about Lewis? I don't know his last name?"

Macon frowned. "Lewis?"

Had Grammy been keeping Lewis a secret? Her grammy? What did that mean? She guessed that if Grammy didn't want anyone to know about her burgeoning romance, she'd keep her secret. It just meant she'd have to be extra careful with her snooping. *Very interesting.* "Never mind," she mumbled, staring down at the note.

"The only Lewis I know is from Cedar Creek." He paused. "Lewis Greer? Retired now? Worked for the state agriculture department? He helped my dad when oak wilt hit the ranch a while back."

She shrugged, feigning disinterest but mentally taking notes. Lewis Greer from Cedar Creek, huh? Now she had something to work with—if she wanted to do a little digging on her grandmother's would-be boyfriend. Who was she kidding? Of course, she wanted to. This was her grammy, after all.

"What other improvements are we talking about?" Macon asked.

She glanced up from the page. "You'll have to wait and see, just like everyone else." Her gaze returned to her grammy's note before his blue eyes and knee-weakening smile could do any damage. *Get it together, Charlotte.* It took three times before the sentence she was reading made sense. Once it did, her stomach dropped. "What decorating committee?"

But the bell over the door rang, demanding she put on her best customer service face for the time being.

"Charlotte." Tabitha Draeger was across the room in a flash, squealing with glee.

"Tabby?" she asked, laughing, as the two of them hugged. "You're here."

"I'm always here." Tabby squeezed. "*You're* here. I can't believe it. But I'm so glad." She released her. "I know you just got here and you're probably too tired and jet-lagged to want to have dinner but—"

"Dinner sounds perfect." When was the last time she'd cooked? Really cooked. It would likely be dangerous to her and Tabby's health. "Out?"

"Yes, of course." Tabby clapped her hands. "Yay. I'd hoped, since it was almost closing time, that you'd say that. Hutchinson's BBQ? Valencia's?"

"Barbecue. I haven't had good barbecue since the last time I was in Texas." And just like that, her stomach started growling.

Macon glanced her way, the corner of his mouth tugging up. "Guess that means I'm free to go?"

Tabby rolled her eyes. "*Please.* You were the one who volunteered to drive me into town."

He had?

He shook his head. "You know I had to—"

"Stop by the fire station for *something*." Tabby nodded. "Can you drive me home, Charlotte? Otherwise, I'm sort of stranded. I'm sure Momma and Kolton would love to see you, too. And you could meet Gwen and the girls, as well."

"Or I can pick you up?" Macon was staring at the counter. Charlotte had spread out a sampling of her favorite photos and postcards, things she carried with her when she was traveling. Since she was staying put for the next ten days, she'd thought about displaying them. Maybe here, in the shop, others might enjoy them, too. Just a few, of course, since her goal was to make the shop a Christmas wonderland.

"I didn't realize you were staying in town?" Tabby asked.

He didn't answer as he moved one postcard aside to pick up a photo beneath it.

"Macon?" Tabby asked.

"I am." He put the photo down, cleared his throat, and nodded. "I have to go over the roster at the firehouse before making sure everything is on track for the toy drive party. That sort of thing." He paused, glancing her way. "Thanks for the cookie donation, by the way."

"Cookies?" Charlotte asked. She did not bake. The few times she'd tried had resulted in an oven fire, a burned-out mixer, and three ruined cookie sheets. After that, she'd vowed never again.

He tapped the lilac folder. "I bet everything you need to know is in here." His blue gaze fell from hers.

"Cookies. For the Christmas Holiday Toy Drive party." She didn't have the best track record when it came to baking. Or cooking of any kind, really. "Hopefully your fire-fighting skills won't be needed." It was a joke... Sort of.

"Right." Tabby nodded. "The toy drive. Now I feel bad. That is a big deal. Sorry for teasing you."

He shrugged, headed toward the door. "Text or call me.

Have fun." And without another word, he left.

One look at Tabby told her Macon's sister was just as surprised by his rapid exit as she was.

"Well, bye then. Love you, too," Tabby called out, laughing. "Brothers."

Charlotte laughed, too. "Only child."

"I'm not going to lie. There are times when that sounds amazing." Tabby's blue eyes sparkled. "It's so good to see you."

"You too. Want some tea? I have some delicious cinnamon orange tea from South Africa." Charlotte headed toward the electric teakettle she'd plugged in behind the counter.

"Sounds yummy." Tabby followed her toward the counter, taking a seat on one of the barstools. "Wow," she whispered, sifting through the pictures, memorabilia, and postcards. "You've done a lot of living in a lot of places."

Charlotte picked up the image Macon had been studying, her heart lodging in her throat. She hadn't meant to bring this one—she hadn't. It was of her and Macon, all smiles, sitting on Grammy's porch swing with the cat he'd found between them. His arm was around her, and she was leaning into him. This one was just for her. Until now.

"Guess that's the one he was looking at?" Tabby asked, taking the picture.

Charlotte didn't answer. It didn't make sense for the picture to upset Macon. It was a happy picture—of happier times. For her, some of the happiest ever. That's why she cherished it so much. Maybe he didn't feel the same? *Don't read anything into it. Change the subject.* She picked up another picture. This one was of her, sitting on the jungle floor, cross-legged, her eyes closed tight while a large male orangutan played with her hair. "It was probably this one. Look at the face I'm making."

"Are you scared or laughing or crying?" Tabby shook her head.

"A little of each. It was pretty intense." She set the photo aside. "In the end, my hair wasn't that interesting and he ran off before I could get any good pictures of him."

Tabby shook her head. "I'd freak out." Her friend set the picture aside and glanced at the one of Charlotte and Macon again. "Funny how things turn out though, isn't it? You're both happy, doing what you love. That's pretty awesome."

"What about you?" Charlotte put a tea bag in each cup and turned, resting her elbows on the counter. This was easier. Talking or thinking about her and Macon was hard. Not how good it had been between them—not that part—but how painfully it had ended. How *she'd* ended it. Had she ever regretted it? Yes. Many times. But they'd been so young, with different dreams and goals. For Macon, family came first. He'd wanted to make his father proud and serve his country and community. While Charlotte had always craved a family of her own, she feared, deep down, she'd disappoint Macon in the long run. She'd been raised as a nomad, always moving, always on the go. She loved it.

They'd both been so young—too young, according to her parents. They needed a chance to live and decide what they really wanted. So Charlotte had ended it.

And we've both moved on, so stop thinking about it.

"Oh, you know, I've just been dealing with wrangling

brothers, and being an entrepreneur." Tabby grinned. "That sort of thing."

Charlotte gave herself a mental shake. No more thinking about Macon tonight. Instead, she and Tabby had a lot of catching up to do. Starting now. "Really? I want all the details."

MACON READ OVER the complaint again, shaking his head. It was anonymous of course. No one wanted to take credit for 'causing trouble.' But he had no doubt the surrounding business owners would be watching, with wide-eyed interest, when he climbed out of the fire truck.

Two wrought iron tables sat, with two chairs each, on the sidewalk in front of Krauss's Blooms. It looked nice. Inviting. Only, according to the caller, it was a clear violation of the city ordinance for blocking the sidewalk—impeding the flow of pedestrians and restricting emergency vehicle access.

Strictly speaking, the caller was right. If he pulled out his tape measure, which he'd be forced to do, he was certain the tables exceeded the allotted space for storefront seating. A bench or a few chairs was one thing. Charlotte's outdoor café setup was a definite no-go. And, as the town's fire marshal, it was his job to inform her of that fact.

Armed with his clipboard, tape measure, and citation pad, he pushed through the front door and stopped short.

Charlotte was on her hands and knees, wedged behind the flower chiller. Fern sat, staring at her, head cocked to one

SASHA SUMMERS

side, waiting patiently.

"I'll be right...with you," she called out.

He waited, more than a little curious to see what she was doing. When it came to Charlotte, life was never dull.

With a groan, she tried to back up. A resounding 'thunk' echoed. Followed by a distressed, "Ouch."

He was moving toward the chiller, sizing up the massive case and how heavy it was. "Charlotte?"

She froze. "Macon?"

"Are you stuck?" He paused, kneeling. "You hurt?"

"Just my elbow." Her voice was muffled. "Just..." she twisted, up onto her knees "...a..." slowly she slid out, pressed tightly against the exposed brick wall, from behind the chiller "...minute." Finally, she was out, sitting on the floor, a tad breathless. "Here." She tossed a rubber bone to Fern.

Fern pounced on the toy, tossing it, then catching it, and running in excited circles.

"Don't you dare laugh." Charlotte stared up at him, rubbing her elbow.

He tried not to, he did, but there was no holding back. "I'm sorry." He held his hands up. But he was also still laughing.

She shook her head, a reluctant smile forming. "Fine. Laugh. She was so sad."

"You realize she's small enough to have crawled under there herself?" he asked, watching Fern chewing on the toy.

"She won't. She's scared of this thing." She patted the front of the chiller. "It makes all sorts of weird noises."

"Because it's old. As in ancient old." He offered her his

46

hand.

"You mean vintage?" she responded, letting him help her.

He pulled her up, the brief contact sending a jolt across his palm and up his arm.

"Thanks," she murmured, stepping away from him.

He flexed his hand. "I think that term applies to clothes and cars only." He nodded at the chiller as it began to click and hiss. "*That* is *old*."

Another louder hiss and alarming grinding sound had Fern picking up her toy and trotting to the other side of the shop.

"I don't blame you, Fern," he said to the dog.

Charlotte straightened her shirt and ran a hand over her hair. "It's a mess, isn't it?" she asked, pulling the band out. She ran her fingers through her long dark hair, smoothing it into place before righting the ponytail once more. Only then did she seem to see him—and his official Last Stand Fire Marshal jacket. "What can I do for you…Officer Draeger?"

Right. Work. He sighed. "I'm here on official business."

"I got that." She nodded. "Am I getting one of the Christmas Ball posters? I think I'm the only one on the block who doesn't have one."

He nodded. "Edda Mae had one. I don't know what she did with it, though." He collected his things from the counter and handed her one of the extra posters.

"Thank you." She found a tape dispenser and carried it and the poster to the front door. "Was there something else?" A few strips of tape later, and the poster was up.

There was no point putting it off. It was part of his job.

"I got a call about the tables."

"The tables?" She carried the tape back to the counter. "They look good, don't they? I thought it was a nice way to keep folks chatting and admiring Main Street, especially with it all decorated. I admit, I love Last Stand at this time of year."

She kept on, looking so happy. So animated. What harm would it do to let her have a few tables? She had a good point—Main Street was all about inviting and keeping out-of-towners around as long as possible. It was good for commerce and all that.

"I had a complaint," he clarified.

"About my tables." Her smile froze. "Honestly?"

"Unfortunately." Her smile wilted. "As nice as they are— and they are—they can't be on the sidewalk."

She blinked, absentmindedly rubbing her elbow. "Because?"

His gaze fell to her elbow—her very red elbow. "City ordinance. Blocking a public walkway, emergency access, impeding—"

"All that?" There was no sign of her smile now.

And, for no logical reason, he felt guilty. He was just doing his job. He had mentioned permits to her before. Still... He wished she'd stop rubbing her elbow.

"I get it." She held her hand up. "I'll move them."

He cleared his throat, staring at his clipboard. It took effort to get the words out around the lump in his throat. "This is a warning. But, next time, there could be a fine." His voice was hard. Not because he was angry with her, but because he was angry with the situation. Not that she'd know that.

"A fine?" she echoed, her voice almost a whisper. "For the tables?"

"For breaking a city ordinance, yes. I'm sorry, Charlotte."

She nodded. "I understand. You're just doing your job."

Right. That's what I'm doing. And crushing your joy. He pointed at her elbow with his pen. "That looks a little swollen. Want some ice?"

"I know this is a warning, but if I was to get fined, how much is it?" She flexed her arm, ignoring his comment.

He caught her wince as she moved her arm. "Forty dollars."

Her nod was slight. Arms crossed, turning slowly on her heel, her narrow-eyed gaze was sweeping the room. She stopped, staring at the chiller, one finger tapping her chin...lost in thought. "How much do you think that weighs?"

"The chiller?" he asked. "A lot."

She shot him a look. "Is that in pounds?"

He grinned. "Why?"

"Oh, nothing." Her barely repressed excitement told him otherwise.

"You can't move that, Charlotte." He paused. "You know that, don't you?"

"I do." She nodded. "And I would never try to, without help."

"Oh, I have no doubt you'd find a way to move it. But I was referring to the electrical outlet. It's not standard." He shook his head. "You don't want to play around with electricity. Trust me on this."

"Fire safety and all that?" She hugged herself, eyeing the massive refrigerated display case. But she didn't look as deterred as he would have liked.

He tried his best to sound stern—like that would change anything. "Promise me, Charlotte." He knew that once she made up her mind about something, nothing stopped her. Hopefully the sheer size of the cooler would deter her. But, with Charlotte, there were no guarantees.

Her lips pressed tight—like she was holding something back.

"I'm serious." He ran a hand over his face. As much as he admired her sheer force of will, this was not the time for her to dig in and be stubborn. "Please."

"Fine," she agreed, but he could tell she wasn't happy about it. Her gray eyes settled on his face. "Is there anything else I can do for you, Officer Draeger?"

He shook his head. "I think we're good here."

Her expression said otherwise.

"Need help moving those?" He paused in the shop door, staring at the two bistro sets on the sidewalk.

"No thank you." She put her hands on her hips. "But thanks for stopping by. And for letting me off with just a warning."

Stubborn. But he couldn't help but smile as he shook his head. "Take care, Charlotte."

Chapter Four

CHARLOTTE STUCK ANOTHER pencil in the bun on the back of her head and rearranged the pictures on her newly purchased corkboard. Since Macon's official visit yesterday, her brain had been working through potential ways to reconfigure the shop. Ways that would open up the floor space so her tables could come inside. Patrons could stay, have tea, buy flowers, and relax. It would be a feast for the senses—and unlike anything in Last Stand.

A flower café. She'd seen variations in Madrid, Osaka, and Gongju—and she'd loved them all.

Her computer chimed. Time to Skype with Grammy.

"Grammy?" She waved.

"Your hair looks like a porcupine." Grammy smiled. "What are you up to? That many pencils mean big ideas. Or big trouble."

"Brainstorming." She grinned. "Where are you? Tell me what you're seeing?"

Grammy filled her in. She'd flown to London, stayed overnight, then boarded her ship. "We're headed for Dublin." She held up a well-worn brochure and pointed at the map. "I can't believe it, Charlotte. I've wanted to take this trip for so long. And now, here I am."

"You deserve it, Grammy."

"How are things there?" Grammy sat back, cutting the top part of her head out of the screen. "Hold on." The camera moved up, then down, then centered again. "Better?"

"I can see you."

"Did you read my note?" she asked.

"I did. You were right—it was more of a novella." She scrunched her nose up. "You could have given me a little heads-up about the cookies. Do you know how long it's been since I baked something?" Making five dozen cookies for the toy drive party was no small thing. "You should remember. It was your mixer I fried, and your oven that caught fire."

Grammy chuckled. "I do remember. Well, that was a long time ago. You were always trying to stray from the recipe, too. Don't, and everything will turn out right."

"If you say so." She didn't share Grammy's confidence in her. And, because the toy drive party was being held at the firehouse, it would mean she'd see more of Macon.

Right now, she'd seen quite enough of him.

"I am confident your cookies will be the talk of the town." Grammy's smile was wide. "If you need some ideas, you know where my recipes are."

But the cookies weren't the worst of it. "What about the charity ball decorating committee?" she asked. "That seems like an awful lot of responsibility for an outsider. Are you sure everyone will be okay with it? Will I even know anyone I'm working with?"

"There's no reason to worry over this. You've always had a good eye, making things pretty—finding the best light and angles and such. That's why every picture you take is so spellbinding. And I don't know a single soul who works harder than you do, Charlotte. They'll be thrilled to have you on board, helping out. I do it every year, dear. They rely on me. It didn't feel right to leave them in the lurch. And I so appreciate you taking my spot." Grammy pointed at the pencils. "Now what's all that about? Some new assignment for your magazine has you all excited? Getting ready for another stamp in your passport?"

She shook her head. What was going on with her job, or lack thereof, would only worry Grammy. There was no way Charlotte would ruin this trip for her grandmother. "It's the shop."

"My shop?" Her surprise was almost comical.

"I have a brilliant idea." She picked up one of the pictures and held it in front of the camera.

"Well, that's lovely dear," Grammy said, leaning forward to stare at the computer screen. "But I'm not sure you should put all that time and energy into my little shop."

"Of course, I should." She held up another picture. "Can't you just see it, Grammy? I was thinking, if you're okay with it, about moving the refrigerator case around, to the far wall? That would open up the floor and make room for some tables—"

"I guess it would." But there was hesitation in her voice.

"If you don't want me to, I'd understand." She paused. "I guess I am sort of forcing my idea on you."

"It's not that, Charlotte. It's a lovely idea." Grammy sighed. "I was going to wait until I got back to tell you this but, well, I've been thinking about retiring."

Charlotte swallowed.

"If I do, I'll be selling the shop." Grammy shrugged. "I'd

hate for you to put all this time and effort into it if that's what I decide to do."

"Sell the shop? Krauss's Blooms?" The instant lump in her throat made it impossible to say more. It was hard to imagine it.

"I don't have the energy I used to." She shrugged. "I'm getting older—"

"You have more energy than anyone I know," Charlotte interrupted. "Don't think about the shop for now. You're on vacation—a well-deserved vacation. I shouldn't have dumped this on you."

Grammy stared at her for a minute. "No, now, you know what, Charlotte? You go ahead. After all, sprucing the place up can only help us get the best offers, right? If I do decide to sell?"

"Right." With any luck, her shop makeover would change Grammy's mind—at least for a little while. Selfish or not, Grammy and the shop were the only constants Charlotte had ever had in her life. "I'll give it all I've got. If you're sure?"

"I'm sure." Grammy nodded. "You go crazy. Make Krauss's Blooms the prettiest flower shop you've ever seen, one that serves only the best teas. Come to think of it, you might want to reach out to Tabby. Her new sister-in-law makes the most amazing pastries and treats. It couldn't hurt to see if she wants to sell some of them in your flower café, too."

"Grammy, if you were here, I would kiss you."

"I'll expect that kiss when I get home." Grammy nodded. They chatted on for a few more minutes. Charlotte reminded Grammy to see St. Patrick's Cathedral when she arrived in Dublin and Grammy reminded her that her oven ran five degrees hotter than it read. By the time their chat wrapped up, Charlotte was more convinced than ever that she could change her grandmother's mind.

Fern placed a paw on her foot, her way of asking to go out.

"Come on then, let's go." She stood, walking across the wooden floor to open the back door. "I bet we could work something out. I'll visit more often and let Grammy do more traveling. We could even take turns, maybe."

Fern didn't seem the least bit interested.

"Well, I think it's a great idea." With a flip of a switch, the back garden was bathed in a pale white light. Charlotte opened the back door and waited on the wide porch, staring up into the endless night sky. No matter where she traveled, the sky always seemed bigger in Texas. She collected her well-traveled camera from inside and headed back out to snap a few pictures, the layers of blue and black creeping across the sky, deep and rich.

This was what she needed—to slow down. She'd been going nonstop, taking every assignment, earning more and more stamps in her passport, and generally wearing herself out. Somewhere along the way, the excitement and anticipation had begun to fade.

Maybe some time here would help her rekindle her love of travel. If not...well, she had time to figure things out.

Fern barked, her tail and ears alert, before deciding she'd fulfilled her guard-dog duty and went back to sniffing the grass. "Good job, Fern. I feel safer already." Not that there was much to worry about in the way of neighborhood crime. Last Stand was lucky that way.

There was so much to love about this little town. Tourists were definitely taking notice, and more and more city folk were making their homes here. This time of year was especially appealing. Draws like the Christmas market, caroling, Main Street and the courthouse lights had more than a few out-of-towners wandering in the shop to look around. She'd made them tea, sold a few poinsettias, and handed out cards to a bride who was convinced Last Stand was the perfect place to have her wedding.

She pulled her phone from her pocket and sat in one of the rocking chairs on the back porch. There were no messages from Jason, and nothing from her coworkers. Radio silence. She'd updated her résumé and sent it to him, like he'd asked. But, this close to the holidays, it was unlikely she'd hear anything anytime soon. At least that was what she was telling herself.

Fern trotted onto the porch and flopped down beside her.

Tomorrow was Sunday and the shop was closed. That meant she had the whole day to start working on making the flower shop into a flower café. But she'd need help and she was counting on Tabby Draeger to give it to her. She found Tabby's number and called.

"Hello?" Tabby answered on the second ring. "What are you up to?"

"Well, I have an idea. If you're free, I was hoping you could help out. Could you come over?" She paused. "And maybe Gwen could come too? I have a business proposition to discuss with you both."

"I think that can be arranged." There was a smile in Tabby's voice. "Can I bring anything?"

"I think I know where Grammy's tools are, so we should be set."

"Tools?" Tabby laughed. "So, no dress and heels?"

"Probably not. But I'd love to try out some of Gwen's pastries. Grammy told me all about how amazing they are."

"That's not a problem. She made some chocolate croissants, some ginger-peach tarts, sour cream Christmas-tree cookies, and—"

"My stomach is growling." It was. Loudly. Poor Fern was sitting up, staring at her in concern.

"We can come now if you want. With food? Save the tools part for tomorrow?"

"Are you sure?" She glanced at her watch. "It's eight thirty on a Saturday night. I don't want to cramp your social life."

"Are you kidding? We're on the way." She paused. "No boys allowed, right?"

"No boys allowed." She didn't know how Macon Draeger, the man, would react to her flower café plans but something told her Macon Draeger, fire marshal, would have a whole lot to say. And frankly, she didn't want to hear it.

"MACON, MACON, THIS one now." Jilly held out a tube of red frosting, icing oozing out the back.

"I think you're getting more frosting on your arm than

on your cookies, Jilly." He grinned, setting the tube aside and wiping the frosting off the little girl's arm.

Amy, Jilly's twin, laughed. "Messy." She wrinkled up her nose.

Macon nodded. "Yes, ma'am. Frosting is messy. But it makes Christmas cookies look yummy."

"Is there a cookie under there?" Kolton asked, shaking red, white, and green sprinkles on top of his blue-frosted sugar cookie.

"Yep." Jilly nodded, holding out her hand. "Still sticky, Macon."

"I'm pretty sure the only way to get rid of all the stickiness is a bath." But Macon rinsed the towel and tried again.

"You were supposed to decorate cookies, Jilly Bean, not yourself." His eldest brother, Lam, leaned over to plant a kiss on his stepdaughter's forehead. "You're sweet enough as it is."

Jilly giggled.

"Here, Jilly." Amy slid her bowl of colored sugar-crystal snowflakes between the two of them. "See?"

He, Kolton, Lam, and Jilly all watched as Amy picked up a single sugar-crystal snowflake and placed it on the same gingerbread man she'd been decorating for ten minutes. To look at them, there was no denying the girls were twins. But their personalities were entirely different. Jilly was loud and funny and prone to making messes. Amy was shy and careful and too tidy for a three-year-old.

"Too pretty to eat." Kolton shook his head. "I think we need to save that one for your momma."

Amy grinned. "'Kay."

"You save one too, Jilly," Lam said, pointing at the cookies buried beneath frosting and sprinkles, red hots, tiny gumdrops, and a few raisins.

"That one," Jilly said, pointing out a solid blue angel.

"Because blue is her favorite?" Lam asked.

Jilly nodded.

"Good call." Macon pulled a clean plate from the cabinet and placed the two cookies side by side. He couldn't help but grin at the difference—just like the girls.

"Bath time," Lam said. "Since Momma is out with Aunt Tabby, I think you need to have extra bubbles."

Kolton and Macon exchanged a smirk. Lam and Gwen hadn't been married six months yet, but there was no denying how complete the bond was. To Lam, the girls were his. Lam loved Gwen and his girls with his whole heart. And, no matter how much grief he and Kolton liked to give their older brother, there was no denying the difference in Lam since Gwen and the girls had joined the family. His brother was a happy man and it showed.

"Bubbles?" Amy clapped her hands.

"Let's go!" Jilly slid from her seat and ran from the kitchen, squealing with glee.

Amy followed, giggling.

"You going to clap your hands, too?" Kolton asked.

"Or giggle?" Macon scratched his chin. "I really want to hear you giggle."

Lam cocked an eyebrow. "I might just giggle, since you two get dish duty." He was grinning ear-to-ear as he left them in the kitchen.

"We're getting the raw end of the deal here," Kolton

said, eyeing the globs of frosting dotting the marble countertop.

Macon's phone vibrated.

"Don't even think about giving me some fireman emergency thing," Kolton barked. "You hear me? Unless there is an actual fire, grab a sponge."

Macon chuckled, reading the text. "It's Frank Harker. He said the lights were on at Krauss's Blooms and there is music playing inside."

"He's texting you, why?" Kolton asked, grimacing as a particularly large dollop of frosting stuck to his fingers.

"Neighborhood watch." Of a sort. Frank was a soft-spoken elderly man with a herd of cats and a large German shepherd. He and his dog walked up and down Main Street every night. He called Macon for every little fix-it job he could think of, from changing a lightbulb to lubricating a squeaky hinge. And if he saw something unusual, like lights or music, he was sure to let Macon know all about it.

"Think he'll still text you when you're in Wichita Falls?" Kolton glanced his way.

Macon shook his head. He'd sent in his résumé as soon as he'd gotten the call from Diego Rivera. But so far, he hadn't heard a thing.

"I'd feel pretty confident if I were you, Macon. They called you. Once the holidays are over, you'll be hearing from them." Kolton picked up the tube of frosting. "Do we throw this away?"

"Do you want to risk upsetting Gwen?" He took the tube, squirted the frosting into the trash can and submerged it into the sink full of soapy water. "Better safe than sorry."

"There you go, always Macon-it-better," he joked.

"I'm making some coffee." Macon ignored his brother's jab. "Want some?"

Kolton nodded. "No second thoughts, about leaving? Now that Charlotte's here?"

"Charlotte will be leaving again, once Edda Mae gets back." Macon continued scooping coffee into the filter. "Not that her staying or leaving would impact my decision."

Kolton stopped. "That's not what Tabby thinks."

Macon groaned. Their sister was known to speak her mind. "Here we go."

"She made a few good points. You've always been the loyal sort—"

"Can we not talk about Charlotte Krauss?" He glanced over his shoulder.

"Why?" Kolton was grinning. "Don't want to admit you're still—"

"You want to drink this coffee or wear it?" He slammed the lid shut on the coffeepot and turned to face his brother.

Kolton was laughing.

"What now?" Lam asked as he came back into the room, his shirt dripping wet.

"Who was giving whom a bath?" Kolton asked.

"The grandmothers rescued me." Lam headed through the kitchen to the laundry room, emerging seconds later in a new, dry, shirt. "Why does Macon look like he's in pain?"

"Because he is a pain." Macon pointed at Kolton.

"That's nothing new." Lam slid onto the stool. "Why is it getting to you now?"

Macon glanced back and forth between his brothers. "Either of you know what Mom wants for Christmas?"

Kolton leaned toward Lam. "Classic dodge maneuver there."

"You struck a nerve, Kolt. A big one." Lam nodded. "Let me guess: Charlotte Krauss?"

Macon ran a hand over his face. "What are we? In high school?"

Lam shrugged. "You did fall for her pretty hard back then."

"And we all know how true-blue Macon is." Kolton nodded.

Macon took in the pristine state of the kitchen, hung the dish towel on the oven handle and walked out of the room without another word, ignoring their hoots of laughter. Whatever they thought, he and Charlotte were over. They'd been over for nine years. Sure, it was nice having her back and, yes, she still caught his eye but…that was all. That had to be all. There was no future for them. How could there be? Even if he wanted one. Which he didn't.

"Macon?" Jilly came running down the hall in her pink fairy pajamas, arms outstretched. "Night kisses."

Macon scooped her up in his arms and planted a kiss on her cheek, making a loud smacking sound and earning a giggle from Jilly.

"My turn." Amy was right behind her, wearing her lavender fairy pajamas. "Me."

Macon shifted Jilly to one side and caught Amy, giving her the same loud smack of a good-night kiss.

"Daddy laughing?" Jilly asked.

"Yep. Daddy thinks he's downright hilarious." Macon

sighed. "Uncle Kolton, too."

Amy rested her head on his shoulder. "Story?"

He headed toward their room, one in each arm. If they wanted a story, he'd read them a story. If the Wichita Falls job worked out, there wouldn't be many more bedtime story nights. "Which one are we reading tonight?" he asked. "The fairy princess one or the fairy ballerina one?"

"Bawaweena." Amy smothered a yawn with her hand.

"Okay," Jilly agreed.

They were both sound asleep before he'd made it past page four. He stared down at the girls, tucking in their girly-girl pink blankets and clicking off the butterfly painted lamp on their nightstand before slipping from the room. Thankfully, their fairy night-light shed just enough light for him to dodge the pile of blocks, the stack of books, and various pieces of dress-up clothes covering their floor.

Lam was waiting in the hall outside. "Thanks."

Macon nodded.

"You're good with them. And they sure love their uncle Macon." Lam grinned.

"What's not to love?"

Lam shook his head. "Hear me out, will you?"

Macon crossed his arms over his chest. "Do I have a choice?"

Lam shook his head. "Gwen makes me happy. The girls make me happy. I want the same for you." He stopped, then shrugged. "That's all. I shouldn't tease you about Charlotte. If you say she's not the one, she's not the one. I'll lay off. I guess we were all hoping, with her being back, you guys could pick up where you left off. And if it worked, you'd have what I have." He clapped Macon on the shoulder before peering into the girls' bedroom. "Coffee is ready. And so is Kolton. He's got a few new Macon-it-better jokes he's dying to lay on you." His sigh said it all.

"Thanks for the warning. Tabby said something about a loose stair out in the barn," Macon said. "I figure I'll head that way and take care of it first."

Chapter Five

"I T SMELLS LIKE oranges," the older man said, sniffing the tea filling one of Grammy's mismatched china teacups. "And...cinnamon? Something else? Sorta like gingerbread?"

Charlotte pushed the plate of gingerbread and bite-sized decorated Christmas cookies toward the old gentleman. "Cloves. Exactly. You've got a good nose, Mr. Harker. You've earned a free cookie."

Mr. Harker's smile melted away his armor of skeptical indifference. His hand hovered over the plate, tempted by the dainty details of Gwen Draeger's holiday treats. Did those details make the cookies taste better? She thought so. It sure did make them look irresistible. "Tough choice, isn't it? They're so pretty, you want to eat them all." Charlotte leaned forward to whisper, "I've eaten three of them already."

That earned an outright laugh from Mr. Harker. "Well, you're a slip of a thing. A few cookies won't hurt."

Charlotte smiled. "I like the way you think."

He finally picked a gingerbread man. A classic—white frosting, red hots, and a few raisins. He took a bite, his clouded eyes staring around the shop, pausing here and there to take in the display of teacups, brightly colored tea advertisements, and postcards. But what had him frowning again was the open socket over the door leading to the workroom.

"Do you have any experience with renovations, Miss Krauss? It's no easy thing." His well-wrinkled brow resumed its deep-set furrow. If the open socket had him frowning, the lattice frame wrapped in twinkle lights hanging over the counter had him downright scowling. "You know this is a historic structure?"

She nodded. Her years of travel had taught her to be self-sufficient and go after what she wanted. Covering the entire ceiling in light-wrapped lattice frames was what she want-ed—to start. Since she'd pictured Grammy's shop as a flower café, she couldn't shake the idea. And, right now, with Last Stand buzzing with holiday cheer, a Christmas flower café would be even better. She hadn't had much time to work on that today. Between one of the churches collecting their poinsettias, the library picking up their wreaths, and a large Christmas corsage order to an eager-looking group of teenage boys, she'd been elbow deep in flowers and curling ribbon. In the last hour, things had tapered off. And then Frank Harker and his large stiff-legged German shepherd had shown up. They'd walked back and forth past the shop four times before she'd held the door open and offered him some tea and cookies.

"You don't like the extra lights?" She stared up at the happy sparkle, smiling at their soft glow.

"How many strands is that? I'm thinking the wiring in this old place won't be able to take the extra voltage." Cookie in hand, he pointed at the metal pipe that ran down the exposed brick wall to the electrical outlet—and the power strip plugged into it. "You need to get an electrician over here to take a look at that." But before she could say anything, he added, "What does Edda Mae have to say about all this?"

All this currently consisted of the frame and the Christmas lights and a broken outlet—that yes, she needed to cover. What would Frank Harker, and the rest of Last Stand for that matter, think when she was done? There would be more than just lights. Ribbons and flowers, pine boughs and Christmas ornaments, maybe even some strands of tinsel? *That's a thought.*

"Does your grandmother know?"

"Grammy knows. She gave me her blessing. She said it was time to spruce the place up." She watched as he set the cookie down and took a sip of his tea.

He held the cup back and stared at the warm liquid.

Elbows on the counter, she waited. Frank Harker was a bit of a grump. A tad opinionated. And adorable. He was just the sort of upstanding Last Stand citizen she needed on her side. More than that, Frank Harker could use the company. His solitary evening walks hadn't gone unnoticed. "Good, isn't it?"

Mr. Harker did an odd shrug-nod-headshake thing.

"What's his name?" Charlotte reached behind the counter for one of the doggy treats she kept there.

"Pat."

Pat's ears perked up at the sound of his name.

"My grandson was real little when we adopted Pat. He was always asking to pat the dog. Pat him, Grandpa, pat him?" His smile was pure love. "Soon, the dog responded to

Pat more than his real name." Mr. Harker took another sip of his tea.

She studied the old man. "That's the sweetest thing I've heard in a long time." She held up the dog treat. "Can Pat have a treat? Doggy treat, of course."

Mr. Harker nodded.

She knelt in front of Pat, holding out the treat. "What was his real name?"

"Cary Grant." He shook his head. "My wife's idea. She thought it was the funniest thing ever."

Charlotte couldn't help but laugh. "Well, Pat is definitely less of a mouthful."

The little bell over the door rang and Macon Draeger walked in, a large plastic container in hand. He looked, as usual, too handsome for his own good. "Evening, Frank."

"Evening, Macon." Frank shook his hand.

"Pat." Macon glanced between Frank Harker and his dog. "Looks like you're both having a snack."

"I forced it on them—both of them." Charlotte shrugged. "What can I do for you this fine evening?"

"Gwen asked me to deliver these." Macon sat the container down. "I meant to get them over here earlier, but the day got away from me."

"Happens more and more, the older you get," Frank Harker said, watching as Charlotte opened the container. "What's that?"

Charlotte held the box out. "Help yourself." Gwen's peppermint bonbons, milk-chocolate and white-chocolate fudge, and more cookies filled the container to the brim.

Frank Harker's eyes went wide. "Don't mind if I do." He

took another gingerbread cookie, identical to the one he'd eaten. "For the road."

"Here." Charlotte handed him an orange-pekoe tea bag. "In case you want another cup later. You and Pat feel free to stop by anytime. It was nice to have the company."

Mr. Harker and Pat took their time getting to the front door. He opened it, turned, and smiled. "Nice chatting with you, Miss Krauss."

"Charlotte." She waved.

He nodded then shuffled out.

She turned to find Macon studying her, his forehead creased and one eyebrow cocked high—as if he was considering something. About her. Something puzzling.

"What?" she asked, running her hands over her hair. Her chest tightened, and her skin flushed beneath his bright blue gaze. He had the most mesmerizing eyes. She sucked in a deep breath, her lungs aching for air. "What's wrong?"

"Nothing." He shook his head. "Frank Harker doesn't take to strangers."

"Probably because most strangers don't feed him delicious cookies and soothing tea." She snapped the lid back on the plastic container.

"Maybe." Macon reached for a cookie.

She pulled the container away. "You can have Gwen's cookies anytime. These are for the patrons. With tea. Tea and cookies and flowers and all that stuff."

"Tea? I could go for a glass of iced tea." He grinned.

"Not iced tea." She rolled her eyes, knowing full well that he was teasing her because of the grin on his face. She knew that grin—that playful, teasing grin.

"What sort of tea do you recommend with a frosted sug-ar cookie?" He opened the container and snatched up a snowman cookie before she could stop him. His look was so victorious, she had to laugh. Which made him smile. And her laugh got stuck in her throat. Because, really, Macon smiling was...well, something.

"Peppermint." The word was a near whisper. "Tea. Pep-permint tea."

"I'll have that. A cup of peppermint tea, please." He sat at the counter, biting into the cookie.

Yes, making tea was a good thing. A distraction. It might keep her from mooning over Macon...and his eyes...and his smile. She spun, focusing on making tea. In no time, she had the kettle plugged in and two fresh teacups—peppermint tea bags inside—ready for brewing.

"How are you settling in?" He turned, taking in her at-tempt to fit the wrought iron café tables inside. "A little snug?"

"Because someone told me I couldn't move that thing." She pointed at the chiller full of flowers.

"Is that the technical name for it?" He glanced over his shoulder at her. "That thing? Here I thought it was a display case? Or a refrigerator, even. Huh." He took another bite of his cookie. "But *that thing* totally works, too."

There was no point in holding back her laughter, so she didn't.

He stood, rubbed his hands together, and walked around the chiller—sizing it up. Peering behind it, where she'd been wedged a few days before, he said, "You could move it into the corner."

"I thought you said that was a no-no." But she was already headed toward the massive cabinet.

"I said you couldn't just plug it into any old wall socket." He stepped back, staring down at her. "But I think there's enough slack for you to move it, a bit, into the corner. It would give you more room."

"More room would be good." She thought about her plans—with tables and room for patrons to sit and socialize over exotic teas beneath sparkly lights and blooming flowers. *Yes, more room would definitely be good.* "Let's do this."

"Hold up," he said, grinning. "While I appreciate your enthusiasm and your belief that I could move it by myself, I can't." He paused, sizing up the chiller again. "Nope. It's going to have to wait. I'll get some guys over here from the station. You can thank them with tea and cookies, too." He paused. "Does tomorrow work?"

It shouldn't surprise her that he'd offer to help. Macon had one of those generous spirits, always looking out for others. But, considering their history and her new rule-breaking activities, she was a little taken aback. But only for a moment. "Tomorrow would be great." She clasped her hands behind her back and rolled up on to her tiptoes, awkward and uncertain. "Thank you."

"You're welcome." He swallowed, and tore his gaze from hers. "Closing time, isn't it?"

She glanced at the large clock hanging over the door leading to the workroom. Six o'clock on the dot. "Yep." Meaning Fern would come trotting down the hall any minute, ready for their walk home and her dinner. "Fern's probably hungry."

"What about you?" he asked. "Hildie's Haus is open."

Good point. If she ate out, she wouldn't have to cook—even if cooking actually meant microwaving some of the meals Grammy had left for her. Also, there'd be no cleanup. It's not like Fern would starve—there was a bag of dog food in the workroom for late nights. "Do they still have milkshakes with real ice cream? And the best chicken fried steak?" Her stomach grumbled.

He nodded. "They do."

"Sounds like a plan." She crossed the room and flipped the sign on the door to closed. "Thanks for the suggestion."

"Sure." He cleared his throat. "We could look over the to-do list for the Christmas Ball, if you're looking for some company?"

Company? She and Macon? Having dinner? At one of the go-to places to eat in Last Stand? Nothing good could come from that. Apparently, her expression showed her concern because his posture stiffened and his expression shuttered.

"I thought…" She scrambled for an excuse. "I'm beat. I figured I'd take something home, to Grammy's? Let Fern run around in the yard while I eat?" Her yawn was pathetic—she was a terrible actor. Then she paused, his last comment registering. "What to-do list? How do you know…?" But she knew. Grammy. "You're on the decorating committee, too, aren't you?" That made sense. Was this something Grammy had cooked up, just to get the two of them to spend more time together? Or was she truly a regular member of the decorating committee and they'd be short without her? More importantly, did she want to know the answer?

"Every year." He smoothed his shirt front and winked. "Part of the whole fire marshal gig. Sort of a big deal and all."

She couldn't help but laugh at his over-the-top cocky expression. But, inside, she couldn't shake the tangle of uncertainty and...excitement that working with Macon Draeger stirred. *No. No excitement.* Something...*else*, sure. *But definitely not excitement.*

"First meeting is coming up." His eyes narrowed. "But you knew that?" His blue eyes swept over her face, watching her. "Tomorrow night."

No. "Of course." She really needed to go back and read Grammy's note more closely—to see what other sort of surprises might be hidden there. "Tomorrow night. Sounds fun." *Great. Just great.*

His blue gaze narrowed and his lips pressed flat, as if he was fighting a smile. Because he knew her—and knew how terrible she was at lying. That's why she didn't do it. Ever.

"Fine. I had no idea." The words came spilling out. "I skimmed her note but...you've seen it. And there were so many anecdotes and Grammy comments tossed in, I sort of stopped really reading it on page ten."

He chuckled. "Bet she has dates and times all buried in there somewhere."

"Right between the story of Fern eating a bee and how to reset the breakers? Or what to do if the water pipes here start making a clanking sound? Or when to water what plants— you know how much she loves each and every one in her garden." Out of everything, that's what Charlotte worried about most—killing her grammy's garden.

Fern chose that moment to trot into the room, her nails clicking on the stained concrete floor. "Sounds like riveting stuff." He knelt, rubbing Fern behind the ear.

There was something undeniably appealing about Macon. Maybe it was his smile? Or his kindness? Or his sense of humor? He could always make her smile.

She sighed, loudly, drawing his gaze her way.

"Not on your top-ten list?" he asked. "The decorating committee?"

Seeing Macon and Fern together, Charlotte suspected her grammy's motives for this trip might have exceeded her desire for a vacation. Her grammy wasn't one to give up on something she wanted—Charlotte had inherited that trait. But what Grammy wanted, what she'd always wanted, was for Charlotte to settle down here. With Macon. And they'd have a family—something Charlotte had never really had but always wanted. Once upon a time, Charlotte would have believed that was possible.

But now?

Fern crossed to her, sat, and looked at her with big copper eyes, her stubby tail wagging.

"Right. Dinner. Guess that's my cue," she said, hoping Macon would take the hint.

"Enjoy." Macon nodded. "I'll see you tomorrow."

"At the meeting." She grinned. "And where is the meeting going to be held?"

"The community center," he chuckled. "You remember where that is?"

With a roll of her eyes, she snapped, "Of course." She

shooed him to the door. "I'm going to lock up, Officer Draeger."

But after she'd closed and locked the door behind him, she stared at Fern and said, "I sure hope you know where the community center is, Fern. Because I have no idea."

"SILVER AND GOLD is the theme this year." Susan Juettemeyer pointed at the screen, her PowerPoint full of images and lists. "These are some of the ideas we're considering."

Macon stood at the back of the room, doing his best to seem interested. If anyone noticed him glancing at the door every other minute, people might jump to conclusions, might think he was looking for someone.

Like Charlotte Krauss.

He glanced at his watch.

"I didn't know people still wore watches," Charlotte whispered as she came up next to him.

He glanced her way. "It helps me stay on time." He glanced at the large clock on the wall.

"Is that a dig? Yes, I'm late. It couldn't be helped." Charlotte stared up at him. "I had a customer. I couldn't just push them out of the shop, you know."

"Guess not." It was hard to hold back his laugh. "I thought you were lost."

Her eyes went wide. "I was *not* lost." Her voice rose just enough to draw the attention of...well, everyone.

"Charlotte." Susan smiled. "So nice of you to step in for Edda Mae this year. We're having you partner up with

Macon, since you two already know each other. And he knows the routine. All right?"

That was news to him. Not exactly bad news, but definitely unexpected.

Susan didn't wait for an answer. Instead, she pointed at the screen again. "As I was saying, we're going with classic silver and gold. And white, of course. We're thinking flocked trees—you know, sprayed with artificial snow."

Charlotte made an odd little noise at the back of her throat.

Susan didn't seem to notice. "And lots of silver tinsel on all the branches—"

Another sound, almost a squeak escaped Charlotte.

"With traditional gold and silver decorations." Susan nodded. "Everything has been purchased or donated already—"

This time Charlotte sighed.

He couldn't stop himself from looking her way. "You all right, Charlotte?" The slight furrow of her brow had him grinning.

"Well, it's just…" She glanced his way, then back at the screen. "I'm fine. It's fine."

He crossed his arms over his chest. "Then what's all the sighing and squeaking for? Because you're fine?"

Charlotte nudged him. "Sh. Seriously, the lady doing the presentation is shooting me a not-so-friendly glare."

Lips pressed tight, he turned to find Susan staring them down—while continuing to go through the table settings, photo booth, lighting, and every other little element that she had, undoubtedly, figured out to the most minuscule of details. Susan Juettemeyer took her position as decorating committee chair very seriously. So seriously that no one had ever stepped up to challenge her.

During the rest of the presentation, he was aware of Charlotte's every twitch. And there were plenty of them. He did his best not to react, but he couldn't resist watching her—a little. Her face was a river of expressions, shifting and ever-changing. She might not be as verbally opinionated as Edda Mae, but there was no denying Charlotte had very strong thoughts on Susan's design ideas. And, from the looks of it, she wasn't exactly thrilled.

Once Susan wrapped up, assignments were passed out.

"Flowers?" Charlotte asked as Susan approached, excited. "Since Grammy has the flower shop—"

"Edda Mae was a dear and ordered all the flowers, but we've got someone else covering the arrangements and placement. I didn't want to assume that you'd be interested in something so important, since you're only filling in." She smiled, then frowned. "Not that we don't appreciate your help. We do, definitely. I meant we tend to put our experienced committee members in charge of the big tasks." Her hands fluttered as she talked. "So, Macon here is in charge of lights and safety. But, mostly, safety." She patted him on the shoulder, handed him his assignment, and walked away saying, "Safety first."

"Safety?" Charlotte's nose wrinkled. "I didn't even know that was considered part of decorating." Her frustration was obvious. And adorable. She was adorable.

"When you get that many people in one place, safety is always a concern." Which was true. And part of his job. But he said it mostly to get a reaction out of her.

"Right. Sure. Well, that's just..." Her sigh seemed to deflate her. "Great."

There was no stopping his laugh now.

She glanced up at him, trying—and failing—to be angry. Instead, her smile took his breath away. Why did he keep on fighting? Nine years or a hundred, her smile would always get to him.

He tore his gaze from hers and stared blindly at the paper in his hands. Why would he open that door? The past was just that: the past. Nothing more. *Nothing.*

"What's wrong?" she asked, stepping forward to peer at the paper. "You're scowling."

"Nothing." He cleared his throat. "I was just thinking about...mistletoe." It was the first word he read on the page.

"Mistletoe?" She glanced up at him. "Mistletoe is a safety concern?"

"It can be. Dogs eating it..." He cleared his throat again, racking his brain for a change of topic. "Why do I get the feeling you're not a fan of this year's silver and gold theme?"

Her eyes went wide. "Was it that obvious?"

"To me? Yes." He chuckled.

"It's just sort of...done." She shrugged. "I'd go bigger—brighter. More colorful."

From the flare of enthusiasm in her eyes, he could only imagine what kind of decorating Charlotte would dream up. He'd seen that look a time or two. In high school, she'd been on every festival, dance, and special event committee. She'd take an idea and run with it, making it a full-on experience. That was why she was such a talented photojournalist—she'd go that step further and, through her words and images, take the reader on her travels with her. But not everyone was as talented as she was. "They have to pick the theme early, right around Fourth of July. After that, it's set in stone. They need plenty of time for donations and supplies. All that. If you're in the area then, you should come to a meeting, toss out some ideas." He paused, nodding as a few of the other committee members said a passing hello.

"I'm not sure it's that easy," she whispered. "That Susan lady seems a bit fierce."

No arguing that. Fierce was exactly the right word for the woman. "Susan doesn't like to leave things until the last minute. She's very thorough when it comes to planning. In a case like this, that's a good thing."

Charlotte nodded. "True. For a little town, I remember Last Stand had big celebrations. It's one of the things I loved most about being here."

"Me, too." His gaze locked with hers. Her eyes had always fascinated him. Stormy, cloudy, and velvet gray, with a hint of blue. Curious. Mischievous. Warm. The sort of eyes it was easy to get lost in. He knew firsthand that was true. Even now, he was getting a little too lost in them.

Her gaze fell from his. "Do we need to go over this?" She waved the piece of paper.

Now? No. He needed some distance or he'd make a fool of himself all over again. He wasn't blind. The good people of Last Stand were more than a little curious about him and his high school sweetheart. Whether Susan Juettemeyer had intentionally paired them for that reason or not, it was going to keep tongues wagging through the New Year. At the moment, there were too many eyes on them. "No."

"Oh." She was looking at him, surprised. "Sure. Of course. Here."

He took their list of duties, careful not to touch her, and nodded. Rattled or not, it didn't feel right to leave so abruptly. "Well, all right then, Ms. Krauss. I'll get you a safety vest as soon as I can."

"Safety vest?" She was frowning now.

"We have to wear safety vests at the ball, in case there's an emergency." He paused, hands on hips. "That way people know we're their go-to if there's trouble."

She blinked, her gaze slowly narrowing. "A vest?"

"The orange ones." He ran his finger across his shoulder. "With the yellow reflective tape?"

Another blink. "Macon Draeger, are you teasing me?" But she was smiling.

He grinned. "Maybe a little."

Chapter Six

"YOU HAVE TO come to dinner. Eating dinner by yourself every night isn't right." Tabby held up the end of the burlap and twine laced with lights.

"I do it all the time." Charlotte laughed, taking the cord from her. "Grammy left me a freezer full of food."

"I'm sure it's good, but I'm talking about Marta and Gwen's cooking. It's straight-out-of-the-oven deliciousness." Tabby pointed at the plate of tarts she and Gwen had brought.

The melt-in-your-mouth tarts had been too tempting to resist. Charlotte had inhaled three before she forced herself away from the tray painted with bright holly berries.

"If you want to come, that is," Gwen added, braiding red, green, and white ribbons together. "I think everyone would understand if you didn't want to."

Charlotte wasn't sure what was worse—that Macon was the reason she wasn't saying yes to a dinner invitation or that they knew he was the reason she wasn't saying yes.

"I wouldn't let it bother me." Tabby shook her head. "You're over him." Then she turned and bobbed her eyebrows at Gwen. "She says she's over him."

Charlotte ignored their banter and took the looped end of the string of lights and stood, carefully, on the next-to-the-top step of her brand-new ten-foot-tall ladder. There'd be no more balancing on furniture or stepstools—no reason for any upset if there happened to be another unexpected drop-in from Officer Draeger. Or any other wandering local fireman…

"Tabby." Gwen's voice lowered, almost apologetic. "People are already talking."

"They are?" Charlotte paused.

Tabby shot Gwen a look. "Way to go."

"I didn't think it was a secret." Gwen's shrug was almost an apology.

"It's not that bad," Tabby argued.

People were already talking? About what? Charlotte hung the cord on the hook that she'd screwed into the wooden beams that ran crisscross across the shop ceiling. "People have too much time on their hands." Did she want to know what was being said?

"It's a small town, Charlotte. And, come on, everyone loves my brother." Tabby laughed. "He's just…lovable."

Macon was one in a million. A good man—a really good man.

"That's true." Gwen nodded. "Any man who will wear fairy wings to read two little girls a bedtime story is *entirely* lovable. He's an amazing uncle."

The image of Macon in fairy wings had her smiling.

"I might have a picture." Tabby pulled her phone out. "Don't tell him. He'd be so mad."

"Tabby." Gwen was shaking her head, but she was laughing.

Charlotte climbed down the ladder, her gaze trained on

the picture. Macon, sleeping, with two adorable little girls draped across his lap—also sleeping. And, yes, there were sparkly pink wings peeking over the top of his broad shoulders. Her chest grew instantly heavier, her lungs oddly tight. She sucked in a deep breath. "How old are they?"

"Three." Gwen started another braid of ribbons. "And busy."

"You haven't met the girls, yet," Tabby added. "Come on, Charlotte. You can't let what people say affect you. Why do you care, anyway? You'll be off having grand adventures again in no time."

Would she? Is that what she wanted anymore? Travel was her passion. The entire wall covered with her postcards was proof of that. But the thrill of living out of a suitcase didn't hold the same appeal that it used to.

"Chances are, you'll both be gone after the holidays." Tabby glanced back at the photo on her phone, her smile dimming.

"What do you mean? Macon is leaving?" It was impossible to imagine Last Stand without Macon. He was...fundamental to this place.

"It's not set in stone," Gwen argued.

Tabby shot her sister-in-law a disbelieving look. "Who wouldn't hire Macon?"

"I don't want to think about it, okay? The girls will be devastated." Gwen expression dimmed. "He's their favorite uncle."

How could Macon leave? This place was his home. "Whatever it is, it must be something amazing for him to consider leaving Last Stand. I remember how connected he's always been to this place—to the land here. How much he loved the ties he could trace back for generations." She broke off, wishing she could stop the words that kept coming. "Is it for a job? Or...something else?"

"Something else?" Tabby smiled. "No, Charlotte, there's no mystery woman luring him away, if that's what you're thinking."

They were both staring at her again, probably because she'd just undone everything she'd been trying to do since she arrived. With one question, she'd put herself back into the 'is-she-or-isn't-she-over-him' category.

Since she couldn't rewind the last few seconds, she opted not to say anything else. Instead, she picked up one of Gwen's finished braids and climbed back up the ladder, threading the ribbons into the canopy overhead. With the addition of ribbons, ivy, and cinnamon stick ornaments, her vision was beginning to take shape. Now all she had to do was finish the dozen pomanders and she'd be satisfied. Maybe. Camera in hand, she took a few pictures. "It's coming together." She nodded, scrolling through her pictures.

"Um, this is amazing," Tabby agreed.

"You're so creative, Charlotte. I've never seen anything like this." Gwen's gaze swept over their handiwork. "Do you have a dress for the ball?"

"I'm not going." Charlotte shook her head. "Grammy will be back by then."

Tabby was staring at her. "And what? You think Edda Mae Krauss is going to skip the Christmas Charity Ball? Or that she'll let you sit this one out?"

"I don't have anything to wear," Charlotte said. "And I'm not going to buy a dress that I'll probably never wear again."

"That's practical." Gwen nodded, a small smile on her face. "But I'm sure Edda Mae will have…an opinion on the matter."

Tabby was laughing. "I can't wait to hear all about that."

Even Charlotte couldn't help but laugh then. Chances were, Grammy would not be okay with her skipping one of the highlights of Christmas in Last Stand. Maybe it was better to give her a heads-up now, while she was an ocean away, so they could skip that drama when she came home.

For the next hour, the three of them worked and laughed, chatting about kids and family and life. Charlotte mostly listened. Listening to the other women filled a hole in her heart. For all her adventures, there wasn't much she could add when they got talking about family. Her parents were, as always, away. It was the one thing she'd never had— roots. That was why she'd come to live with her grammy when she'd gone to high school. Yes, Grammy had put her foot down about it, but Charlotte was thankful for those four years.

Leaving for college had been one of the hardest things she'd ever done.

And coming back that first summer? Seeing Macon?

The weight on her chest intensified.

Stop. There was no point in rehashing any of that. Not again. Whatever past they had, their future held friendship. They were both entirely different people. Well, she was. Macon was still Macon. Bigger and manlier and all that but... *Not going there.* Right. As Grammy said, 'Best to face a problem head-on.' Macon wasn't the problem. But the way she was reacting to him was. If Grammy was right, all she had to do was look him in the eye and let go of the past. Easy. Simple. No big deal.

"It's really amazing." Gwen stood, staring up at the ceiling. "If my girls ever visit, they'll think you have fairies in here."

"Bring them." The twinkle lights peeking out between the ivy and holly did have a magical quality about them. "Once it's all finished, we can have a fairy tea party."

Gwen stared at her. "I don't know. They might never leave."

She packed the scissors and ribbons behind the counter. "Thank you, both, for all your help. I'm sure this isn't the way you guys wanted to spend the last few evenings."

"I'm loving the girl time. And, hello, look what we've made." Tabby pointed at the ceiling, then hugged her. "You're a creative genius. We are so going to talk about this for some upcoming weddings I have booked at the ranch. If you decide to come to dinner, you can see the barn. That's where we have most of our wedding receptions. Maybe you can even suggest some decorating ideas—things we can incorporate into our wedding packages." Tabby held her at arm's length. "And if you really don't want to have dinner—"

"I'd like to." And she would. As long as Grammy's philosophy worked and she could get over this awkward nervousness Macon Draeger's presence triggered.

"Really?" Tabby was wide-eyed.

"Really?" Gwen echoed. "Tomorrow night, then. I'll

make something special."

"Don't you dare." Charlotte shook her head. "It's just me, joining you for a family dinner." The word family struck a chord deep inside her. It was familiar. An ache—one she spent more time ignoring than acknowledging. Family.

Maybe, while she was here, she could pretend she was part of theirs.

SOMETIMES, HE HATED being fire marshal. And this was definitely one of those times. Macon shook his head. This wasn't going to be fun. But it had to be done. He'd just head in there, lay down the law, and leave. It was his job to enforce the restrictions the city council and community had agreed upon to help preserve the authenticity of Last Stand's historical district. Normally, it was a job he enjoyed— because he loved his town and wanted to preserve it, in all its glory.

But normally his work didn't involve Charlotte Krauss. Specifically, fining her for yet another breach of a city ordinance. If it hadn't been right there, staring him in the face, he'd try to find a way around serving her a fine. As it was, he had no choice.

He didn't open the truck door, didn't look up from his clipboard—wishing, for the first time, this wasn't part of his job. But it was and, like it or not, Charlotte was breaking the rules. As much as he admired Charlotte's desire to make her latest dream come true, she had no idea about the proper way to go about renovations, let alone the permits that had to be in place before work could be done. Especially on a historic downtown building.

Her neighbors did.

And they had no problem making sure he knew about it.

Now he stared out at the freshly painted window frame and door and frowned. She hadn't applied for a permit to make exterior improvements to the building. If she had, she would have been given the list of approved colors.

He wasn't here to serve her one fine. Nope. She was getting two. Considering she'd already been warned once, she was quickly earning a reputation as a rabble-rouser. *Always the rebel.* A smile tugged up the corner of his mouth.

The knock on the hood of his truck made him jump.

Lam stood there, looking at him, his black felt hat tipped down, fleece-lined jacket buttoned up against the surprising northern wind that had blown into town this morning. For Texas, it was downright wintry.

"Pondering the meaning of life?" Lam asked, once he'd rolled down the window.

"I wish." Macon shook his head.

Lam's brows rose. "That sounds all kinds of ominous."

He held out his clipboard.

Lam read it over and, if possible, his brows went higher. "I don't envy you. Shame, since it looks nice." He handed back the clipboard, his gaze sweeping the shop picture windows up and down the street. "I bet you've got an audience, too. It's better than watching one of those reality shows."

"Thanks, Lam, for making this even better." Macon climbed out of the truck and slammed the door, tugging his jacket closed and zipping it up. "What are you in town for?"

"A little last-minute Christmas shopping." He nodded at Krauss's Blooms. "I figured I'd get Gwen some flowers, while I'm here."

He nodded. "I hear husbands do that from time to time."

"Good husbands." Lam grinned. "I've heard tell a man who's courting has been known to buy flowers for his intended, too."

Macon shot him a look. "I'll make sure to share that with the next courting man I meet."

"Sticking with denial, I see." Lam nodded and glanced at the shop. "Going in?"

With a sigh, Macon got out of the truck and headed toward the shop, Lam right behind him. The scent of fresh paint unmistakable. He opened the door, and the little bell announced their arrival with cheer.

Charlotte was the epitome of holiday spirit from head to toe. Her hair was braided back and tied with red ribbon. Christmas bell earrings swung from her ears. Her black dress was covered by a red-and-white striped candy cane apron. *Pretty as a picture.*

He took a deep breath. Peppermint. Ginger. The place smelled like Christmas.

She was animatedly talking to a couple sitting at one of her café tables, sipping tea. A few of Gwen's tarts had been served up prettily on mismatched china. And a colorful patterned rug covered part of the concrete floors, creating a warm, cozy atmosphere. She'd managed to infuse the shop with a welcome and warmth it lacked. Framed pictures, pressed and dried flowers, and what looked to be pages from books hung throughout. The café tables were covered in brightly printed scarves. And overhead...? He stared up, hands on hips, and blew out a slow breath. He'd never seen anything like it. Charlotte had turned Edda Mae's little flower shop into something...fanciful.

And he was proud of her—for her vision and the work she'd put into it to make it come true.

If he could overlook the overloaded power strip to the hot plate sitting behind the counter, he would. But he wasn't wired that way. No matter how pretty it looked, there were more violations here than he cared to add up. And, for her sake and those of her guests, it was up to him to make sure things were not just warm and welcoming, but safe.

Lam nudged him, making him all too aware of Charlotte's gray gaze narrowing at the sight of his clipboard.

"Lam," Charlotte gushed, hugging his brother. "Good to see you."

Their reunion hadn't been nearly so warm, Macon thought. She hadn't hugged him like that, or been happy to see him. It shouldn't have bothered him. But it did.

"You too, Charlotte." His brother nodded, rocking back on his heels as his gaze swept the shop. "I like what you've done with the place."

Go ahead. Make me into a bigger jerk. Unofficially, he liked what she'd done, too. *Liked* wasn't the right word. Marveled? She'd done this. Created an atmosphere of fantasy, of magic. An escape. It was...exceptional.

"Well, I know it's different." She shrugged, smiling. "But different can be good, right? Your wife and sister have been my partners in *crime*." Her gaze met his and she waited, her arms crossing over her chest.

He cleared his throat. "Charlotte—"

"*Officer* Draeger." Her jaw tightened. "The clipboard tells me this is an official visit. What dire offenses have I committed this time?"

He sighed. "The paint out front." He cleared his throat, her steady gaze making it hard to go on. "The city preservation board has specific colors approved for use. And only after the appropriate permit and applications have been filed." He handed her the paper with the list of infractions and the fines.

Her eyes went round. "Wow." Her nose wrinkled. "Well..." She stared at the paper. "I guess, this isn't too bad—"

"Well." He paused, clearing his throat again.

"Well?" she repeated, her smile faltering. "There's more?"

He glanced at Lam, fully aware that his brother was fighting back a smile. "Weren't you going to buy some flowers for Gwen?" he asked.

Charlotte blinked, then nodded, turning her attention to his brother. "What are you thinking, Lam? Special occasion?"

"Don't need one." He grinned. "Just a nod to how appreciated and loved she is."

Charlotte lit up at his brother's simple honesty. "That so sweet, Lam Draeger. Gwen's a lucky lady."

He nodded. "I'm a lucky man and I know it."

She shook her head. "Well, then. Let's see what I have..."

Macon waited until the two of them were busy assembling a bouquet for Gwen before he began making a list of potential fines. He slipped into the back workroom and froze—another exposed outlet. The fuse box was missing its door. The steady drip of the work sink had him down and peering under the counter. The pipe was near corroded. From his spot on the floor, he stared up at the ceiling overhead. A large spider crack in the far corner, on the same wall as the fuse box, meant possible foundation shifting.

"I'm not sure I want to know what you're doing." Charlotte stood staring down at him.

"Trying to save you and Edda Mae some money." He sat up, wiping his hands on his jeans.

"Oh." She held her hand out. "Well…then I guess I should thank you."

He took her hand and stood, denying the urge to hold on a little longer than necessary. And fighting the urge to brush the curl that had slipped from her braid away from her cheek.

"So, thank you." Her voice was soft.

He nodded, his throat too tight to answer. The sensation of being anchored, right there, grounded by the weight of her gaze, was unshakeable. As long as she was staring up at him like that, he wasn't moving. Breathing was a little challenging, too.

When she knelt and peered under the sink, it was a relief…and a disappointment.

Her voice was high. "I'm guessing it's bad?"

He sucked in a deep breath. "It's not good." He squatted at her side.

It wasn't part of his job to walk her through the shop pointing out the various infractions, and potential dangers hidden, and not so hidden, in Krauss's Blooms. But it was the right thing to do. Her passion for this place was inspiring—he didn't want anything taking that from her. Taking her smile. But that's what he ended up doing anyway. By the time he was done, the shop was empty and her smile was long gone.

"In short, yes, it's that bad." Charlotte flopped down into one of the café chairs. "I don't think Grammy has any idea."

"Probably not," he admitted. "Honestly, maybe it's a good thing I got these calls."

The disbelieving look on her face almost made him laugh. Almost. He figured now was not the right time.

"I mean, at least now you have some warning, and you can have things fixed before something happens. Something potentially serious." He sat across from her, smiling as Fern uncurled from her bed beside the counter and trotted across the floor to his side. "Isn't that right, Fern?"

Fern stretched, her tail wagging.

Charlotte sat forward, resting her elbows on the table and her chin in her hands. "You're right. That's good. Especially if Grammy does..." She broke off, her gaze bouncing from him to Fern to the brilliant illuminated flower canopy overhead.

"Edda Mae does what?" he asked, rubbing Fern behind the ear.

She shook her head, a deep 'v' forming between her brows.

As much as he wanted to push her, he knew better. If she didn't want to talk about it, she wouldn't. Still, he didn't like the way she drooped in her seat, almost defeated.

He leaned back in his chair and stared up at the flowers. "You did this?"

She hesitated. "If I say yes, will I get a bigger fine?"

He chuckled.

She laughed, too. "Yes. With Tabby and Gwen's help." She tilted her head, her eyes locking with his. "But if that means they'll get fines too, I'll say I forced them—against their will."

He shook his head, still smiling. "I'm not going to fine you for this. You did good, Charlotte. This, all of it, you did really good."

Her smile was back. Bright and warm, rolling over him and pressing in until his lungs were empty. "Thank you."

Her gaze held him in place, making him wish for a time and place that no longer existed. Back when Charlotte had been his world and they'd shared everything. With her, life had been better—complete. Now, they lived in very different worlds.

She glanced at the clock. "Closing time." She stood, smoothing her hands over her apron. "I guess I need to get a handyman in here. I'll ask Edda Mae about that tonight."

"You're talking to her?" It shouldn't surprise him—they were close. Charlotte always said her grammy was the one person she could count on to be there for her.

"Every week. No matter what. She loves Skype."

He stood. "Tell her I said hello." He headed toward the door.

"I guess I'll see you in a bit." She held the door open. "Tabby and Gwen invited me to dinner."

And neither of them had thought to give him a heads-up? Why would they? He'd been the one reassuring them, over and over, that he and Charlotte were just friends. And they were. Period. Friends. "Oh, well." Dinner with Charlotte and his family. "I'll see you at dinner, then." *What could possibly go wrong?*

Chapter Seven

"CHARLOTTE, DON'T BE silly." Grammy shook her head. "How will it look? You've come all this way to help me out, and then you miss the Charity Ball? The Charity Ball I've forced you to help with? Between running the shop and all these improvements you're making, people will think I've worn you out."

"Grammy…" She bit into a carrot stick, starving. At midday, two large groups of tourists had come through. She'd made tea, sold all of the treats Gwen had supplied, and a good supply of her cinnamon stick candy cane air scents and mistletoe pomanders. All in all, a good day. But there hadn't been time for lunch. "I don't think so."

"Well, I know so." She frowned. "You are going. I still have all of your old things from high school. Your dresses, too."

Charlotte laughed. "I am not wearing a prom dress to the Charity Ball."

"I don't see why not if you don't have time to buy something new." She shook her finger at the screen. "Besides, there are some perfectly lovely dresses in there. I remember one that was all pretty and pink and lacy with puffy sleeves."

Charlotte shook her head, remembering the dress all too well. "Um, I'll look." She leaned forward. "The shop needs a few more substantial repairs than I expected."

"Oh?" Grammy paused.

She went through the list Macon had drawn up, watching her grammy's reaction. But there wasn't a hint of surprise on her grandmother's face. "You knew?"

"Of course." She nodded. "I only trust MD Repairs, Charlotte. I mean it, no one else—the others are all after money and do shoddy work. This sounds like something that can't be put off any longer. Electrical wiring is nothing to mess around with. The card is at the shop, pinned in the back room. I just wasn't sure it was worth investing my money into, since I'm thinking of selling—"

"Grammy, you can't sell. You can't. Krauss's Blooms is a staple on Main Street. And, now, you should see the changes I've made. Tabby and Gwen really want to do some exciting stuff with weddings...and, well, you just can't." Charlotte told her all about her week, their sales, and the upcoming wedding Tabby wanted her help with. "So you see, there's a solid income stream there."

"I do, sweetie, and I appreciate your hard work. But making the shop more profitable won't allow me any time off."

Charlotte nodded. "I was thinking about that. Would you consider a partnership? I'll work a few weeks, then you do? We could rotate, as well as hire one or two good part-time workers."

Grammy sat back, her head tilted. "I guess I could think about it."

The surge of relief that shot through Charlotte was totally unexpected. "You will?"

Grammy nodded.

"Thank you, Grammy." She could breathe a little easier. "So, tell me about your cruise."

They spent the rest of their chat talking about the trip highlights. Charlotte gave her a few more must-see suggestions and signed off by blowing her a kiss.

Fern, who'd been staring at the screen from her spot on the bed, sat up.

"Miss her?" Charlotte asked, scratching her behind the ear. "She'll be home soon—just five days," she promised the little dog. "And then what, Fern? Christmas and New Year and then... What am I supposed to do if Grammy doesn't agree to this partnership?"

Fern licked her hand.

"Thank you for the support." She slipped off the bed and stared at her reflection. From her limited collection, she'd decided her black dress was appropriate. At Grammy's suggestion, she was borrowing one of her grandmother's holiday pins and her holiday bell earrings again. It was Christmas, after all.

Once Fern had a treat and she'd loaded the Draegers' gifts into her grammy's lilac van, Charlotte headed down the sweet streets of Last Stand to the country road that led to Draeger Ranch. She knew the route like the back of her hand. How many times had she made this drive? Too many to count.

It wasn't just Grammy who had made her time here special. The Draegers had, too. They'd opened their doors and their hearts to her, and welcomed her in.

Macon especially.

From the first day of high school until she'd left for college, they'd been inseparable. He'd taught her to ride a horse. She'd dragged him to every museum within a day's drive—it had taken her a while to realize just how big Texas was. But the drive, all the laughter and fun, had been some of the best parts. Time together had never been wasted time. She had cherished every moment she'd had with him. She still cherished those memories.

By the time she was pulling into the driveway leading to the ranch, it was hard to shake the sense of nostalgia.

The large ranch house, its windows glowing in the deep dark of the night, welcomed her back. Armed with her centerpiece, she walked to the door and—

"I saw your headlights." Tabby was holding an adorable little girl with copper curls on her hip. "Jilly and I wanted to say hello."

"Hello." Charlotte was in awe over the wide-eyed girl staring up at her. "It's nice to meet you, Jilly. I like your curly hair."

"Hi." Jilly nodded, pushing up her glasses. "Thank you."

"Come on in." Tabby stepped aside. "Did you make that?"

She nodded, handing her friend the centerpiece she'd made. "I was playing with ideas last night. It turned out pretty nice. There's a spot for a candle, too, but I didn't have one."

"It's so pretty." Tabby led the way into the great room. It was exactly the way she remembered it. "Next year, if for some reason Edda Mae takes another trip, you should come earlier and set up a booth at the Christmas market. I bet you could sell these, along with the wreaths and cinnamon stuff Edda Mae normally sells."

"And some of the holiday pomanders, too?" She saw Tabby's confusion. "The flower balls with the ribbons?"

"I know what a pomander is." She adjusted Jilly. "I'm just a little surprised you didn't instantly shut me down about being here next year."

But Mrs. Draeger appeared, followed by Kolton and Lam, Amy and Marta, and all the hugs and hellos saved her from having to come up with an answer. She'd forgotten how big and loud and wonderful this family was. This is what she'd missed most. Even though she wasn't a Draeger, when she was here, she felt like one.

"You didn't have to bring us anything," Adelaide Draeger said, shaking her head at the bag full of wrapped presents.

"It is Christmas," Charlotte argued.

"It's very thoughtful of you." The older woman's blue gaze searched hers. "You've always been so thoughtful. It's so good to have you home, Charlotte. You've been missed."

Had she? It was something people said, to be polite. But it was nice to hear, all the same. That her absence had been noticed, mattered.

"You got here just in time." Gwen poked her head out of the kitchen. "The roast is perfect and the potatoes are nice and crispy on the outside. Macon set the table, so it's his fault if the silverware is wrong."

"I heard that," Macon called from the other side of the massive great room. "I know how to set a table. I think."

"Can I help?" Charlotte asked.

"Just talk to Mom," Tabby urged. "She'll love hearing all about your travels. It's been hard for her, since Dad's passing."

Charlotte glanced at the older woman. While Joseph Draeger hadn't exactly been the most effusive of men, he'd loved his family above all else. And he and his wife had had one of those bonds that made even the biggest skeptic believe that love existed. Of course, it would be hard for her, now that she'd lost the person she'd shared more than half of her life with. Charlotte couldn't imagine such a loss. Couldn't imagine such a bond... But she wanted to.

Macon was lighting the candles that lined the middle of the dining room table. It was set to perfection.

"Looks okay," Kolton teased.

"It looks lovely." Mrs. Draeger shot her son a disapproving frown.

"Can we add this?" Tabby held out the centerpiece. "Charlotte made it."

Macon inspected the holly and ribbons, antique glass Santa, and glitter-twisted twine. He didn't say anything, but his look—his smile—said enough. Why his approval mattered was still a mystery, but it did. And a flush of pleasure washed over her to see him rearrange the table and put her creation front and center, adding a large red column candle. "Like this?" he asked.

"Lovely," Mrs. Draeger said again. "Sit, please."

"I hope you didn't go to all this trouble because of me," she whispered as Macon pulled her chair back for her.

"Nope," he whispered back. "We always eat by candle-light on our best china on a Wednesday. It's a family routine." He winked.

She laughed and sat, watching the chaos that ensued as Jilly and Amy were settled, after changing seats four times, and the food was served.

"I hear you've been making some changes to Edda Mae's shop?" Mrs. Draeger asked.

"Just a few—with her blessing, of course." She took a bite of perfectly crisped roasted potatoes. "Oh, Gwen, these are amazing."

"A few changes?" Lam chuckled. "I'm not sure Edda Mae will recognize the place when she gets back."

"It will be more familiar when I repaint it." She shrugged.

Gwen frowned. "But we just—"

"I messed up." Charlotte cut her off. She wasn't about to let Gwen or Tabby take the blame for her ideas. "I didn't know about the guidelines and rules and… Well, I painted when I shouldn't have, and it was the wrong color. So I need to fix it."

"Macon," his mother spoke up. "Surely, you can do something to help Charlotte out? After all the work she's done to spruce up the little shop, it seems foolish to do something all over again."

The slight tightening of Macon's jaw was hard to miss.

"I don't mind." Charlotte assured her. "It was my mistake. I tend to rush headlong into things when it comes to something I want. And changing everything isn't always a good idea when it affects a historic main street. I need to get permits first, follow the rules."

"Which doesn't come easy to you." Tabby grinned.

"And Macon can't exactly help, Mom, since he's the one giving Charlotte all the fines." Kolton laughed.

"What?" Adelaide Draeger was horrified.

"It's my job, Mom."

"But…it's paint." She frowned. "What does that have to do with—"

"That's Macon. Paint Patrol." Kolton was still laughing. "Frank Harker has him on speed dial. I bet he's the one who outed Charlotte for all of her violations."

Poor Macon was practically squirming in his chair now.

"I'm actually relieved. Mr. Harker is just a concerned citizen, after all. I'm sure he meant well. If Macon hadn't stopped by, I wouldn't know about some of the real issues that need fixing." She smiled at him. "Thank you, again."

"Aw, Charlotte, you shouldn't let him off so easy," Kolton moaned.

"Be nice, Uncle Kolt," Amy chastised.

"Yup," Jilly agreed, patting her mouth with her napkin.

Adorable. Charlotte couldn't help but smile. *Absolutely adorable.*

"Good girl." Lam nodded, pressing a kiss to Amy's forehead.

And, once again, Charlotte was touched by the closeness and love of this family. These little girls held the heart of everyone at the table. Charlotte could see why. While Amy's words had been to reprimand Kolton, her shy smile and wide-eyed interest in everything was enchanting. Jilly was more animated, keeping up a constant conversation with anyone who spoke to her.

The ringing of a cell phone drew all eyes around the table.

"It's not me." Kolton held his hands up.

"Me, neither," Lam said.

"We have a 'no phones at the table' rule." Tabby paused. "Macon, of course, is the exception."

"Excuse me." Macon stood. "I need to take this."

"Everything okay?" Lam asked.

Macon nodded as he left, his booted footsteps echoing as he walked across the great room and out the back door, leaving Charlotte to wonder who and what the phone call was about.

MACON LEANED OVER the bed of his truck the next day, and listened to the voice mail.

"Hello, this is Charlotte Krauss. I'm in charge of Krauss's Blooms and I'm in need of an estimate on some rather significant repairs. My grandmother, Edda Mae, said you were the only one she'd let do the work so I'm hoping you might be able to stop by sometime soon and take a look? Please?" She left her number and said thank you again.

He grinned.

Charlotte had no idea he was the MD in MD Repairs.

Edda Mae, I know what you're up to. It might have escaped Charlotte's notice, but he saw exactly what Edda Mae was doing—playing matchmaker.

He shook his head.

It wasn't like he hadn't thought about it—them. The more time he spent with Charlotte, the more his heart ached for her. But loving someone meant putting their needs and wants first. And the one thing Charlotte wanted, what she'd always wanted, was the freedom to travel. It was in her blood, cultivated by her parents' nomadic lifestyle, and her passion for photography. If that was what she still wanted, he wouldn't hold her back.

But her interest in the shop gave him hope.

Why would she spend so much time and energy transforming the shop? It wasn't for Edda Mae. Charlotte's grandmother made sure the place got a coat of paint every now and then, but she'd never said a word about making the sorts of changes Charlotte had made. Which meant, this—all of this—was Charlotte.

That had to mean something.

It might even mean that maybe, what she wanted had changed…

And if there was even the smallest glimmer of hope that that was the case, he'd be a fool not to do everything in his power to convince her to stay. Nine years hadn't changed a thing. He loved her the way he loved her then, with every part of him. To him, she was the only woman who belonged in his heart. Charlotte Krauss had always been the one for him. Then and now. Always.

"What are you grinning at?" Kolton asked, leading his horse Ajax into the barn.

"Nothing." He put his phone in his pocket and opened his toolbox, making a mental checklist of everything he'd need to get started at Krauss's Blooms. He'd have to order a few things but—

"What was the phone call about last night?" Kolton slid

the saddle from his horse and rested it on the rack against the wall. "It was about the job, wasn't it?"

He glanced at his brother. "They offered me the job."

Kolton frowned, then smiled. "Congratulations, I guess? I mean, I get it, I do. But, it's hard to imagine not seeing your ugly face around here. And it means I'll be stuck in those fairy wings more often, to make up for you not being here."

Macon shook his head. "Maybe."

"What does that mean?" Kolton hung the saddle blanket on a peg and faced him. "I thought this was a done deal?"

"I asked for a little more time." He closed the lid of his toolbox.

"Because?" His brother's expression said it all. And Macon braced himself for the teasing to come. "Let me guess? The same reason you spent more time smiling and staring than eating at the dinner table last night?"

"It is Christmas, Kolt." Which might not be the whole truth, but it was reason enough. "It doesn't feel right, up and leaving right now."

"That's a good reason not to leave right away but not a good reason to delay accepting the job." Kolton tipped his hat back on his head. "I get it, man. It was nice having her back here last night. And I know you've never let anyone else in—not like you did with her. But, Macon, what if she leaves—"

"What if she stays?" he interrupted. He was holding on to that tiny thread of hope with both hands.

"Has she said she's staying?" Kolton leveled a hard stare his way. "I don't want you losing out on something big. You know a job like this doesn't come along all that often, Macon."

Neither did a second chance at happiness.

Everything his brother said was true. And, if he was being honest with himself, they were all the things he considered before asking for more time. Saying yes? It just didn't sit right with him. Not yet—not if there was a chance for him and Charlotte. "I thought you said you'd miss having me around."

Kolton shook his head, smiling. "I would. I'm your brother. But it's my job to look out for you." He paused. "I just want you to be happy, man."

"Don't get all emotional on me, Kolt. I haven't had enough coffee for that." He opened the truck door. "I've got a repair call."

Kolton shook his head and went into the barn.

Before driving to Krauss's Blooms, Macon stopped at the hardware store to pick up a few things he knew he'd need. He parked out front, loaded up his toolbox and headed into the flower shop to find Charlotte standing on a stepstool, stretching to screw in a lightbulb.

"Charlotte." He shook his head.

She looked exactly like a kid who'd been caught with her hand in the cookie jar. She stood on the step, bulb in one hand, pointing at the bulb with the other. "It's burned out."

He sat his tool bag on the floor and crossed the room. "Let me." He held his hand out.

"I...I have a ladder." She shrugged. "I guess...this was easier and... It's burned out."

"I know. And I know you don't like waiting on things."

He nodded, waiting for her to climb down before taking her place on top of the stepstool. "I'm just glad you didn't fall this time."

Her sigh was hard to miss.

"You can sigh all you want." He screwed the bulb in and climbed down to face her. As adorable as she was, she needed to understand she was taking unnecessary risks. And he didn't like it. "But your safety matters… Safety matters." He cleared his throat, the words hanging there between them.

A slow smile spread across her face.

A surge of warmth blossomed in his chest. "Better?" he asked, glancing at the light.

"Thank you." She nodded, still smiling. "Are you here in an official capacity? I don't see your clipboard."

"I don't need my clipboard this time around." He shrugged. "But I am here for work."

Her smile dimmed. "Um…I'm confused."

He laughed. "For the repairs. Edda Mae didn't tell you? MD Repairs."

"Tell me?" She was frowning—until her gaze found his tools. "No. MD—"

"Macon Draeger." He pointed at himself. "That's me. But you knew that part."

Her eyes pressed shut. "My grandmother has an odd sense of humor."

"No arguing that." He nodded. "But, since I know what we're looking at, I can just dive in. This is what I've worked up so far," he said, handing her a piece of paper. "The real hazards are at the top of the list—the things that can wait are further down. I won't know what sort of foundation or wiring issues we're looking at until I get in there and look around."

She nodded, reading over the list. "Okay then. Well, Repairman Draeger, where do we start?"

He shook his head. "I've got this."

"But—"

"Really." He nodded at the stepstool. "I might need to borrow this, or your ladder, but otherwise, I'm good."

"I'm just supposed to stand around and do nothing—"

He was laughing again. "Charlotte, I'm not asking the impossible."

Her eyes narrowed, but the hint of a smile played on her lips. "I'll take that as a compliment."

The door over the bell rang, calling her to work and giving him the chance to head to the back and assess the crack before replacing part, if not all, of the fuse box. In order to do that, he'd need to turn off the power, so he'd have to wait until closer to closing time for that. And since he'd have to crawl under the building to look at the foundation— something he *really* didn't want to do now—he moved on to the next item on the list: the faulty plug.

It was worse than he'd thought. The wiring was probably fifty or more years old, all knob-in-tube, exposed and live...and beyond dangerous. He frowned, then walked back into the shop, and unplugged the power strip.

Charlotte jumped up from her seat at the counter. "Macon—"

He glanced at the customers inspecting the boxes of imported teas she had for sale and shook his head. It was probably not the best time to tell her just how dire the wiring situation was. With any luck, his expression conveyed that.

Charlotte kept her mouth shut, but her eyes flashed all the same.

He winked—he couldn't help it—and headed back to the leaky pipes and new fittings. Since the wiring and foundation were on hold, the plumbing was all he could do for now. He was just finishing when Charlotte appeared, a cup and saucer in her hand. "What's wrong?"

"The wiring's bad, Charlotte. It's exposed and *really* old. Wiring like that has caused many a house fire." He pointed at the door. "It just feels like tempting fate to overload the system this way."

"Meaning?"

"The place needs to be entirely rewired. And the shop needs to be shut down for that, Charlotte. It probably should be shut down anyway, just from code viol—"

"Code violations?" She slumped into one of the folding chairs next to the work counter. "Maybe Grammy's right."

"About me being the best handyman in town?" If teasing could take some of the sting out of the news, he'd try.

She rolled her eyes. "No. And, for your information, she did *not* say you were the best handyman in town." With a sigh, she continued, "Only that you were the only one allowed to work on the shop."

He sat in the chair beside her. "Same thing, isn't it?"

She crossed her arms over her chest.

"I know this is a lot, but it's manageable. Don't get discouraged. Look at all you've done already. I'm sure you'll still be able to fix this place up the way you want it, in time."

But he could tell something was wrong. And he had a feeling it was more than just the repairs.

Her gray eyes searched his, considering. "I'm... Yes. I know you're right." But there was no hint of renewed enthusiasm. She leaned forward, resting her elbows on her knees and covering her face with her hands. "I guess this is all a little overwhelming. The shop and the renovations and the fines. I had a vision but not a plan... I didn't stop to do the research first. If I had, maybe I wouldn't have..." She broke off, glaring at him. "And Grammy expects me to actually *go* to the ball? Why? And I still have to bake cookies... I don't bake." She held her hand up. "But I'm not a quitter, even though I'm sorely tempted to ask Gwen to make them for me. I'll figure something out."

He nodded. "I know you will."

"You do?" she asked, sitting a little taller.

He nodded. "It might not happen overnight, but we'll get them done." He'd be more than willing to help her, if she asked—not that he was all that great in a kitchen. But he was willing. "Still, you should go to the ball, Charlotte. Edda Mae will be back, so you could go with her. It would make her happy, if nothing else." He grinned. "I won't even make you wear a safety vest."

Her smile was back. "And the cookies?"

"That sounds like a serious problem." He shrugged. "But if you're going to make them, and you want them to be edible—"

"Macon!" She pushed against his shoulder, but she was laughing.

How he loved the sound of her laugh. "You should come

out to the ranch." He held up his hand when she started to argue. "I know two little cookie elves that would love to help you bake. Gwen and Tabby are supposed to be making cookies for the toy drive as well, so you might as well come out and join in."

"Gwen did offer to teach me how to bake. And if I brought all the supplies, it would still be like I made them, right?" She shot him a look, but there was still laughter in her voice. "Fine. I give up. On the cookies. As for the shop, if you say this is manageable, I trust you." Her gray eyes met his. "I always have."

Macon nodded. "That's a good place to start."

Chapter Eight

"I HAVE THREE recipes." Gwen placed the cards on the large marble counter. "Sugar. Gingerbread. And holiday monster cookies."

"Ooh!" Jilly clapped her hands. "Yum."

"Which is the yummiest?" Charlotte asked, eyeing the long list of ingredients on each card.

"Monster," Amy and Jilly said in unison.

"Then I guess we'll make the holiday monster cookies." Charlotte took the card. "I didn't know there was such a thing."

"It's like an oatmeal raisin cookie dough with all sorts of holiday favorites mixed in." Gwen pointed at the array of bowls she'd already assembled. "White chocolate chips. Peppermint puffs. Red and green candy-covered chocolate. Pretzels and oats." She pressed a kiss to each of her girls' heads. "They love mashing it all together. And the name."

"Monster." Amy made a scared face.

"Monster!" Jilly made a scowl-y face.

Charlotte started laughing. "Well, let's make some monsters. And, considering my talent in the kitchen, let's hope things don't get too terrifying."

"Ooh, yea, I remember your cookies. They *were* bad." Tabby shook her head. "I'll take sugar?"

Gwen nodded. "Gingerbread is my favorite anyway. Plus, I promised I'd make a gingerbread house with the girls, so I don't see why we can't do that while we're at it."

"A gingerbread house?" Memories rushed in. "That takes me back. Every year, well every year I was here, Grammy and I would make one." She measured out the flour, letting the girls dump it into the mixing bowl. "The whole kitchen smelled delicious." Next came baking soda. "Careful with this stuff," she said to the girls. "Don't want to use too much. Trust me on this."

Gwen and Tabby laughed.

"Only do what it says." Charlotte held up the card. "Word for word." Baking soda. Salt. Sugar. Brown Sugar. "This is going to be super sweet."

Amy nodded, chewing a red-and-green candy-coated chocolate.

"Taste testing?" she asked the little girl.

Amy held one up to her.

"Yes, please." She opened her mouth and Amy popped it inside. "Yep, this will work."

Amy giggled.

When the dough was done, Charlotte stared at it. "It looks…edible."

Gwen peered over her shoulder. "Why wouldn't it be? Recipes usually guarantee success."

The girls were having so much fun breaking the pretzel rods and peppermint puffs into smaller pieces that Charlotte pulled out her camera—she carried it everywhere—and started snapping pictures. In their matching holiday aprons, all giggles and joy, the girls were too precious to resist. She set the camera aside long enough to get the tray into the oven, but picked it up, now and then, capturing the joy in this moment.

"More mashing." Jilly had a handful of candy in each hand when Macon walked through the door.

"Whoa there, little britches." Macon scooped her up. "Making monster cookies? My favorite-ist cookie in the world?"

Jilly's squeal and Macon's laugh had an immediate impact on Charlotte. He was good at this—being an uncle. It was obvious the girls adored him. Why was he leaving? He seemed happy enough... When his blue eyes met hers, she lifted her camera and hid behind her lens to take more pictures.

"Is it?" Amy asked.

He nodded. "It's one of them."

"Because Uncle Macon is a cookie monster," Tabby teased. "If you don't watch him, he'll eat them all up."

"Help," Amy said, grabbing Macon's arm and tugging him close. Which brought him to stand right next to Charlotte—smashed against her, actually.

"Hi. Fancy meeting you here, Ms. Krauss." His eyes sparkled. "Don't tell me you made this dough? Is it safe?"

"I was going to offer you the first one out of the oven, but now I'm not so sure." She whispered to the girls, "Should we give him a cookie?"

Amy and Jilly peered up at their uncle.

"Yup." Jilly nodded.

"Yes." Amy grinned. "Yes, yes."

Charlotte sighed. "Guess I'm overruled." She straightened and looked up at him. "You can...have...one."

He was staring at her, an odd expression on his face. For a moment, she thought he was going to reach for her. His hand sort of hovered between them—not moving. His gaze swept over her face, lingering on each feature long enough to make her heart beat faster.

It was all too familiar. Nine years seemed to melt away, pulling the past into the present. She had loved him, *really* loved him. It hadn't been some juvenile crush, but something deep and real that bound them together. And he'd loved her. All she—or anyone—had to do was look at him to see that. His eyes had said so much... And they were saying those same things again. She didn't realize she was holding her breath, waiting, until the oven pinged and they both jolted apart.

"Cookies are ready," the girls said at the same time.

She looked around. Gwen and Tabby, the girls, as well as Lam and Kolton were all in the kitchen—watching her and Macon. She only wished she knew what he was thinking.

"Great." She spun away from him and headed to the oven, pulling the door open—

Macon grabbed her arm. "Hot pads."

Way to make this ten times more awkward. "Thank you. Hot pads. Right. Safety first." She stepped aside so he could pull the large tray from the oven.

"Watch it, fairy princesses, hot tray." He placed the tray on the opposite counter, away from little fingers, and closed the oven door.

Her heart was hammering in her chest. And it wasn't just because she'd almost reached into a three-hundred-and-seventy-five-degree oven with her bare hands. It was because he'd rattled her so much that she hadn't even realized she was doing it. For a man who prided himself on safety, he seemed to be doing his best to distract her.

"They look perfect, Charlotte," Gwen was saying. "You ladies did a perfect job."

Charlotte forced a smile and inspected the tray of cookies. "Looks can be deceiving."

"I'm going in." Macon picked up a cookie. "It's hot."

"You should wait until it cools," Kolton suggested. "But if you want to go ahead and melt the inside of your mouth, hey, who are we to stop you?"

"It's not that hot," Macon argued.

"I can see the steam." Lam shook his head.

But the more his brothers poked, the more Macon dug in his heels.

"Blow," Amy suggested. Her cheeks puffed out as she blew.

Jilly waved her hands. "Careful."

"Got it." He blew the cookie, then took a bite. He chewed, carefully, making all sorts of ridiculous faces before he swallowed. Somehow, he managed to turn one bite into a big production. But the girls were giggling and, yes, she was laughing too—because he was charming and eating a ridiculously hot cookie, just to make her feel better.

And not only her. The girls, too. It was obvious he loved to make them laugh.

"That was..." He paused, eyeing the tray. "The very best holiday monster cookie I've ever had."

Amy stared at her. "Wow."

"Hear that?" Jilly asked, equally impressed by her uncle's praise.

"I officially pass the holiday monster cookie baking duties off to you from now on, Charlotte," Gwen said. "Congratulations."

"Really?" Charlotte was skeptical. Macon was, after all, Macon. He'd always been sweet and supportive—meaning he'd never hurt her feelings. He'd never tell her that her cookies didn't taste good. So, she had to find out for herself. She took a tentative bite from one of the massive cookies and chewed, carefully. "It is edible."

Her trepidation made everyone in the entire kitchen laugh.

"Better than edible, don't you think?" Macon asked.

"You're right." She nodded, beyond thrilled. "These are good. Really good."

"I told you." Macon shook his head, those blue eyes on her face.

"You're also very nice—" She broke off, once more aware of the large and curious group watching them. "You're right." She broke a cookie in half and gave a portion to the girls. "What do you think? Should we get more of these in the oven?"

At some point, Gwen carried the girls off to bed, Lam and Kolton headed back out to work on the ranch, and she, Tabby, and Macon were left to finish off the baking.

"You're closing the shop?" Tabby asked.

"For the next couple of days." She and Macon had worked out a plan. "Macon has an electrician friend who's familiar with old wiring coming in this afternoon. Hopefully, he'll be able to get started. Yes?" She glanced at Macon, and he nodded. "Hopefully it will all be done by the time Grammy comes home. I need to wow her."

"There's no doubt about that, Charlotte." Tabby kept cutting shapes out of the dough. "It's kind of hard not to be impressed with all the work you've done."

But Macon had stopped decorating the gingerbread men. "Need to?"

"She's thinking of retiring. And selling." Saying the words out loud made her tense up again. She didn't know what she would do if her grandmother sold the shop. "Of course, I understand she needs to do what's right for her, but...Krauss's Blooms is the only real home I've ever had. I love Grammy's little cottage, but we spent most of our time together in the shop."

The sympathy on Macon and Tabby's faces was genuine.

"I love that place. I love knowing, no matter where I am or what I'm doing, that it's there for me—with Grammy and Fern and... That sounds selfish, doesn't it?" She paused, pressing pretzel bits into the dough.

"It's not selfish to want a home." Tabby shook her head. "I think it's in our nature to need security, a place to relax and be ourselves?"

"That's it, exactly." Charlotte nodded. "That's how I feel when I'm here, why it's so hard to leave."

"So why do you have to go?" Macon asked, his voice deep.

And that was the million-dollar question. For the first time, there was nothing pulling her away. Before, there had been her job, but it had also been an excuse. She'd left Last

Stand because she'd been afraid. As much as she wanted roots and a family and love, she didn't know how to do any of it. The idea of having that, everything she'd ever dreamed of since she was a little girl, and messing it up? That was far worse than traveling all over the world, so busy that keeping these impossible—beautiful—dreams at bay was easy.

Admitting that to herself wasn't easy. There was no way she'd share it with anyone else. Not yet. Instead, she turned the tables on Macon. "I could ask the same of you? I never thought I'd hear talk of Macon Draeger leaving Last Stand."

His brows rose. "Talk, huh?" His gaze darted to Tabby.

Tabby didn't look the least bit guilty.

"A job?" she asked.

He nodded. "A good job."

She waited, the peppermint puff pieces she held turning sticky in her palm. "It must be. I remember you saying there was nothing that would ever take you away from your home." It was one of the reasons she'd ended their relationship. As much as she wanted to think they could make it work—that *she* could make it work—the fear of letting him down, of hurting him, was greater. "It's hard to picture you anywhere else."

He was staring at her. "Sometimes things change. A fresh start. A new place. You know all about that."

"Not really. My assignments took me all over. But it was never like starting over someplace. I wasn't anywhere long enough to be anything but an observer." She cleared her throat and went back to pressing bits of candy into the dough. "The longest I've been in one place was here. With you." Which sounded oddly intimate, so she added, "All of you." She finished decorating the tray and slid it into the oven.

"Where are you headed next?" Tabby was piping frosting onto some already baked cookies.

"No idea." She picked up a new bag of frosting. "Need a hand?"

"Thank you." Tabby grinned. "How much advance notice do you normally get with your assignments?"

"It varies. Sometimes I know where I'm going to be for six months at a time. Other times, they call and I go running." She paused, smiling. "It's exhausting. That's why I'm thinking about taking a break."

Macon's head popped up, but she ignored him. Somehow, she worried his reaction would impact her decision-making process a little too much. And, right now, that was the last thing she needed. Since Grammy had told her about selling Krauss's Blooms, an idea had taken root, one she wasn't sure what to do with. Travel was in her blood—there was no way she could ever give it up entirely. But her love for the little shop had only grown since she'd arrived. Sure, there were quirky sounds and nosy neighbors and all sorts of city ordinances she'd need to brush up on but...her future was wide open. And she had a lot to think about.

Including Macon.

"I think you deserve a break." Tabby nodded. "Enjoy having air-conditioning and hot water and a roof over your head and, maybe, hanging out making cookies with the people who love you." She nudged Charlotte. "You have something right there." She pointed at her cheek. "I'll get it." With a grin, she rubbed a streak of yellow frosting across

Charlotte's cheek. "Oops."

MACON CRAWLED OUT from under Frank Harker's porch, a small, mewling kitten in his hand. "That's the last one." He placed the kitten in the box, smiling at the four little balls of fluff nuzzling close to their mama. "She was probably just looking for a place to warm up. There was a bunch of dryer lint and what looks like a kitchen towel under there."

"A blue-and-white one?" Frank nodded, chuckling. "I thought I saw her sneaking it out of the kitchen window. She's real fast." He regarded the stray cat and kittens with affection. "She's real skittish most times. But when I come out to feed her, she'll sit by my chair as long as I don't try to touch her. I can respect that."

Macon sat on the step, the box full of felines between them. "Seems to me like you two have an understanding."

"Guess we do." He nodded at the cat, affection in his voice. "Glad she let you get to them. I'm sure she knows we're only trying to help her out."

"Me too." He grinned as Pat sniffed the outside of the box. "I'm glad you called. It's supposed to get down to freezing tonight."

Frank nodded, eyeing the cat and her kittens. "We'll make room for them inside. Won't we, Pat? Here's hoping Momma Cat won't mind too much."

Pat sat, his ears perked up, staring at the box.

"Poor dog—an old man and a bunch of cats for companionship." He chuckled. "But we get by."

"I haven't heard any complaints." Macon grinned, rubbing Pat's head.

"You been spending a lot of time with Edda Mae's granddaughter." That was Frank, straight to the point.

"Yes, sir, I guess I have. As you know, there's more than a little work to be done in her shop—"

"Don't try to pull the wool over my eyes, boy." Frank was grinning. "I know what you're up to and, if you'll take advice from this old man, you need to hurry things along. Edda Mae won't be gone forever."

It was Macon's turn to laugh. "You like Charlotte, then?"

"What's not to like?" He shook his head. "Funny and stubborn and kind and opinionated and full of ideas. You'll never be bored, that's for sure. No man wants to live a boring life."

Macon chuckled again. "I'd have to agree with you on that one."

"What's the holdup then?" Frank asked.

"She's been back in town for a week—"

"And Edda Mae will be back when?"

Macon swallowed; time was ticking away. "In three days."

"Three days?" Frank Harker shook his head. "You got a lot to do in three days, son. You best get a move on."

Macon was still reeling from the older man's blunt assessment of the situation. "I'm curious now. What does 'getting a move on' entail?"

Frank's disappointment was plain to see. "That little shop, for one. She's turning it into a jewel box. You help her finish that. And take her out, son, make her feel special." He leaned closer. "In my day, taking a young lady's hand meant something. There's caroling tonight. And it's going to be a cold night. Hands get chilly."

Macon nodded.

"Where is your gal now?" he asked.

"The shop is closed while the place is being rewired, so she's supposed to be at home." He glanced Frank's way. "Which means she's probably at the shop." He stood up, dusted off the front of his jeans and stared into the box of kittens. "I'll carry them inside before I go. I'm sure they'll like it better where it's warm." As long as Momma Cat didn't panic and make a run for it.

She didn't. She was all purrs and contentment when Macon set the box down in the living room, to the right of Mr. Harker's recliner. Pat's bed was on the left side. Mr. Harker brushed aside any further attempts at small talk, but finished by telling Macon to stop wasting time.

A short while later he pulled up at Edda Mae's cottage and found the van parked. She was home, after all. Then he drove on, heading for the shop. Mr. Harker might not be too far off. While Ned and his boys were working on the wiring, he could get Kolt over, to help him move the case and get whatever else he could knocked off her lists.

Kolton wasn't exactly thrilled about Macon's call, but he showed up and, between the two of them, they managed to move the case as far into the corner as possible.

"I didn't expect there to be this much room." Kolton surveyed the additional space. "She'll like it."

Macon nodded. Knowing her, she'd have another table and chairs set up in no time.

"Anything else? Since I'm here?" Kolton stared around the shop. "I haven't been here in a few years, but I'm thinking this is all her idea? Where did she come up with all this?"

"It's called a flower café. She said she'd been to a few—in places all over the world. It's all about the scent, flowers and tea." Kolton was looking at him. "What?"

"Oh nothing." Kolton shoved him. "You've got that look. The same one Lam gets when he's talking or thinking about Gwen. It's sort of nauseating."

Macon pushed him back. "Let's get to painting."

"Great." Kolton stared at the exposed brick walls. "What?"

"Outside. I picked up a color close to the one she wanted, only this one was on the historical approved list." He shook his head. "If she gets fined over this one, it'll be on me."

They spent the next couple of hours painting. Kolton filled him in on the progress he and Lam had been making with the breeding program the ranch was developing with the pro-rodeo circuit. Good stock animals were hard to come by, so the brothers hoped using tried-and-true bloodlines for bulls and broncs would be a lucrative investment. Only time would tell, but both Kolt and Lam seemed optimistic.

Then talk turned to Christmas. Macon had done most of his shopping, but Kolton hadn't even started. Between the two of them, they came up with a few ideas.

"Now all you need to do is go shopping." Macon shook his head. "You know, Christmas comes the same time every year."

Kolton nodded. "I do, indeed. Last-minute shopping is

one of my most beloved traditions."

"Speaking of traditions, are you going to join in on the caroling tonight?" As much as he loved his brother, having Kolt around would make it that much more awkward for him to spend time with Charlotte.

"The only time I've ever gone caroling was when Mom made us." Kolton glanced his way. "Let me guess, you are?"

"I'm thinking about it." If he didn't go caroling, he'd have Frank Harker to answer to. "But first, we have to crawl under the shop to check on the foundation."

"This day just keeps getting better and better." Kolton ran a hand over his face. "You're going in first. I'm not coming face-to-face with whatever varmints have taken up residence under there."

But it wasn't that bad, thank goodness. After crawling around with flashlights, the only thing he and Kolton discovered was a six-foot-long snakeskin. Luckily, its original owner was nowhere to be seen. After Kolton headed home, Macon touched base with Ned, the electrician replacing the shop's wiring.

"I should be done tomorrow afternoon." Ned shook his hand. "It's a pretty straightforward job. But I'm not going to lie and tell you things weren't bad. There was no insulation at all around those wires."

"I appreciate you taking the job on such short notice."

"Are you kidding me?" Ned grinned. "My mother-in-law is in town for the holidays. This was the perfect excuse to get me out of the house. I owe you, Macon."

After walking through the shop with Ned, he made his way down Main Street to Hildie's. He picked up a strawberry milkshake, Charlotte's favorite, and headed to Edda Mae's cottage. He heard Fern barking as he walked to the garden gate. It stuck, requiring him to lift and jiggle before it swung open.

"Oh, Edda Mae..." he sighed. All she had to do was call him, day or night, and he would have come over to fix that gate.

"What did you do to the gate?" Charlotte called from the front porch. "It was fine—never stuck or needed jiggling or anything." She was wearing a Creekbend High School T-shirt, some sweatpants, and her hair was in a sloppy bun with a hundred pencils sticking out of it.

Macon laughed. "I noticed that."

Fern came racing across the yard, circling him, her little nose sniffing like crazy. Between the kittens and crawling around under both Mr. Harker's house and the flower shop, he could only imagine the scents Fern was picking up.

"You're all dirty." She watched him walk up the path, her feet encased in bright pink kitten slippers.

"I am." He held the milkshake out. "That's why I won't come any closer."

She stared at the milkshake.

"Strawberry." His brow kicked up. "Extra whipped cream."

"For me? Macon, you didn't have to..." Her eyes lit up. "But I'm glad you did." Her hands took the cup, the brief brush of fingers and hands sending a full-on shock down his spine.

"Nice slippers." He grinned.

"You know I'm a cat person." She shrugged. "No offense, Fern."

Fern was still sniffing his pants.

"She doesn't seem to be offended." He sat on the bottom step, angling to look at her. Fern was climbing all over him. "Go on, sniff away."

Charlotte sat on the top step, resting her back against the railing. "What brought you into town? I don't see your fire marshal jacket or the dreaded clipboard." She unwrapped her straw and poked it through the plastic lid.

"I think I've forever changed the way you'll look at a clipboard."

"I think you're right." She took a long sip. "Mm. You want some?"

He shook his head. "All yours." His gaze wandered along the white picket fence. In spring, Edda Mae's garden was the most vibrant on the block. She planted wildflower seeds from a local farm, so her yard was a carpet of bluebonnets.

"It's so peaceful here," Charlotte said. "Not as quiet as the ranch, I know, but still, it's nice."

"Not too quiet?" He glanced up at her, the pencils sticking out of her bun catching his eye. "Doesn't that hurt?"

"What?" She reached up. "Oh. Making lists. The more lists, the more pencils."

"That's a lot of lists." What sort of lists? Hopefully they wouldn't mean more official visits for him to Krauss's Blooms—with his clipboard.

Her gaze met his. "I have a lot on my mind." She seemed to be studying him—looking for something.

"You want to talk about it?" he asked.

She opened her mouth. "No. Not yet."

He nodded and stood. "I'm going to fix that gate."

"Macon, you really don't have to do that," she argued.

"I'm here. She'd call me, eventually." He headed back to his truck, collected his cordless drill, rifled through his toolbox for a hinge he hoped would work, and carried it back. He crouched, moving the gate back and forth. "The bottom hinge is okay. But the top one's pretty well worn out." He grinned up at her. "Lucky for you, I've got one that will work."

She shook her head. "Fine. Maybe you are the best repairman in town. If not the best, the most prepared?"

"No, you were right the first time. Best in town." He loved the smile on her face.

"Did you know Grammy has a beau?" she asked. "I did some poking around today and discovered her master gardener Lewis has gone on vacation." She stirred her milkshake with her straw. "A cruise."

Macon stopped drilling. "Lewis Greer?"

"It has to be. The odds of another master gardener named Lewis on a cruise in a community this small are pretty slim." She shrugged.

"He's a nice guy. Good for Edda Mae." He nodded. "How are you feeling about that?"

"I'm happy for her." She wrapped her arms around her legs, her milkshake resting on her knees. "She's been alone a long time and that's not right, you know? Grammy has such a big heart. So much love to give."

"Some people like being on their own." He finished replacing the hinge by hand, worrying the drill would end the conversation—and that was the last thing he wanted.

"I guess." Her sigh drew his gaze. She was studying him again. "Do you?"

He sat back on his heels and looked at her. "Not especially."

Her gaze didn't waver. Even though there was a sizable yard between the two of them, it was as if the world revolved around just the two of them. His pulse was racing and his breath grew uneven. He couldn't look away. Didn't want to.

"Are you free tonight?" he blurted, his heart in his throat.

"Did I forget another meeting or—"

"No." He stood, crossing the yard to stand at the bottom of the steps. "No meeting. I thought you might want to go caroling?"

Her eyes widened and the straw slipped from between her lips. "Caroling?"

"No?" He shrugged. "Not a fan of caroling?" He blew out a long breath. "We don't have to—"

"Yes." She stood suddenly, two pencils sliding from her hair. "I'd like that."

He was smiling like a fool. "Good. I'll be back in a couple of hours. After a shower." He looked down at his dusty clothes, waiting until she nodded. "Good."

"Okay." She was slowly spinning the milkshake in her hands. "Guess I should change, too."

"I'm fine with you wearing those." He eyed her pink kitten slippers. "Talk about making a statement."

She rolled her eyes. "Right."

He finished packing up his tools and turned to wave good-bye, her smile and awkward wave pulling him back in time. That shirt. This porch. How many nights had they spent cuddled up on that porch swing? Those were memories he treasured. And he realized that Charlotte played a part in most of his best memories. Now, he had a chance to make more.

Chapter Nine

CHARLOTTE NEVER THOUGHT she'd be happy to see her old clothes. Edda Mae's dryer was slow so it took forever to dry. And she'd just done a load of laundry and everything she owned was still too damp to wear. So she had no choice but to rifle through the clothes she'd left behind. She always chided Grammy for holding on to things, but now she was thankful. In her room, she found jeans and T-shirts—typical teenage attire—but there were also a few button-down blouses, two sweaters, and her favorite gray flannel shirt, soft from wear.

"I'm going on a date," she said to Fern.

Fern lifted her head off the bed, cocking it to one side.

"I know, I'm in shock, too." Jeans and a flannel shirt seemed like the perfect thing to wear for caroling, since it was on the chilly side. She found her old lined denim jacket too, in case the temperature dropped even more.

A glance in the mirror had her slamming on the brakes.

"Bad idea." This had been her favorite shirt in high school, and she'd worn it a lot. He might remember that.

But the knock on the door told her she was out of time. *It's just a shirt.* Fern led the way to the front door, barking up a storm.

She opened the door to find Macon standing there, all

tall and manly in his black felt hat. If possible, he seemed taller than before. And more handsome. "Hey, sorry, Fern likes to think she's a fearsome protector."

Macon's gaze swept over her shirt. "That's familiar." His voice was thick.

"Edda Mae's dryer is on the fritz so...I had to unearth this thing." She crossed her arms over her chest. The shirt was definitely a bad idea.

"Still looks good on you." He did an odd shake of the head. "Hildie's Haus? Everyone meets up there, does a loop, and comes back for hot chocolate."

"Or, maybe another milkshake? Let me get Fern settled." She waved him inside, then went to the pantry for a treat. "Grammy has her trained—spoiled, but trained. When she's going to be left alone, she gets a treat." She walked out, carrying a dog biscuit. "And she totally recognizes the word 'treat,' too."

Macon was looking at the mess she had spread across the table. Most of it was photographs from her latest trip. "You have a good eye." He tapped a picture of an older woman from the Ayoreo tribe. "That. That look. World-weary but hopeful. It's something people remember."

She glanced at the picture. "You just described her. She was hopeful, and thankful. Hope is universal, I think. I was there tramping through the forest to trail after a bird and she offered me some water."

"Where was this taken?"

"Bolivia." She moved the pictures around. "I think I took twice as many pictures of the people and region than I did of the bird. Wait... Here's the little guy." She offered him the photo. "A black-hooded sunbeam. He's related to the hummingbird and is only found in Bolivia."

"Bolivia?" Macon looked at the picture, then her. "You've been all over."

She nodded. "I've lived my dream."

"My Guard unit shipped me a few places." He shrugged. "Nothing as tropical or as pretty as this. It didn't take long for me to miss being back home." He shrugged. "Guess I didn't get the travel bug."

"It's not for everyone." At the moment, the idea of packing up and hitting the road held absolutely no appeal for her.

His blue eyes bounced off her shirt to her face to the photo in his hand. "You ready?" He turned all the way around, searching—

"Fern took her treat to bed." She slipped on her coat.

He paused again, giving her the once-over. "To look at you, Charlotte Krauss, I'd think we were sixteen all over again." The spark in his eyes was bright and the smile on his face gentle.

"Is that a bad thing?" Beneath his steady gaze, a burst of warmth rose from her stomach to her chest.

He shook his head, his hand rising to smooth a lock of hair from her shoulder. With a sigh, he shook his head. "No. Not at all. But we better get a move on or they'll start without us."

She nodded, more than a little breathless. Camera bag in hand, they set out. The sky was clear, with a crescent moon and a million brilliant stars. "I always forget how big the sky is here."

"No city lights to wash it out." He nodded. "There's

nothing like a Texas sky."

Which made her wonder about this new job of his. "Will you have to leave if you take this new job? I'm still trying to wrap my head around the idea of you not being here."

"You're not the only one. It's only a couple of hours down the road." He shrugged. "Wichita Falls. It's a bit bigger than here—big enough to have a fully staffed fire-house."

"Oh." She swallowed. She didn't want to think about a Macon-less Last Stand. He did so much for so many people, it was who he was. "No more MD Repairs?"

He shook his head. "No need."

Then the job was a promotion, which was a good thing for him. "That's good. Isn't it?" She stepped off the curb and crossed the street, trying to gauge his reaction, something that would be easier to do if they weren't walking along in the dark. "You don't seem excited, Macon."

He glanced at her, brows rising. "No?"

"No." She shook her head, wishing she could see him more clearly. This was a big deal—didn't he get that? Not just for him, but for a lot of people. "Shouldn't you be?"

Another look, this time lingering. "Who says I'm not?" The corner of his mouth kicked up.

"Um, I do." She shook her head, spotting the crowd gathered outside of Hildie's Haus. "And once we're done spreading holiday cheer all over town, we're going to finish this conversation."

"Oh, we are?" He paused, smiling down at her. "Why is that? Why is my level of excitement so important to you?"

Why indeed? She blinked, suddenly thankful for the

shadows. Otherwise, he'd see the fire in her cheeks and the waver of her breath. "Because."

He put his hands on his hips. "That's not a reason."

"Because I want you to be happy." And even though it wasn't a shocking or overly telling revelation, it felt like it was. She made an odd squeak before turning and hurrying to join the crowd of carolers. *Not in the least awkward. Way to go, Charlotte.*

Two blocks and several rounds of 'We Wish You a Merry Christmas' later, she was still having a hard time meeting his gaze. What she'd said was true. Macon deserved the best in life. But he didn't seem all that happy about this great opportunity—not really. She knew Macon. Maybe not as well as she had, but well enough. He wasn't one to hold back. That applied to every facet of his life, from work to family and everything in between. Maybe that's why his subdued behavior was setting off alarm bells in her head.

"Charlotte," Tabby called out, holding Jilly and Amy's hands. "Fancy seeing you here."

Charlotte laughed. "How could I resist? I can't carry a tune, but that's not going to stop me from singing Christmas carols."

"Loudly and off-key," Macon added. "But her smile makes up for it."

"Hey." She nudged him. "This was your idea."

"I'm not complaining." He nudged her back, smiling.

"Uncle Macon." Jilly grinned, holding out her hand.

"Hey Jilly Bean, where are your folks?" Macon bent and scooped up his niece.

"Momma tired," Jilly said.

'Christmas shopping,' Tabby mouthed. "I wanted some time with my favorite-est nieces in the whole wide world," Tabby said. "And I knew there would be hot chocolate after the caroling so..."

"Sing!" Amy jumped up and down.

"Yes, ma'am." Charlotte nodded. "The louder, the better." She fluttered her eyes at Macon.

He laughed again.

"'Jingle Bells'?" Susan Juettemeyer wasn't just the decorating committee chair; she was also the caroling leader.

Surprise, surprise.

She was even more surprised when Amy took her by the hand and tugged her to the front of the group. Apparently, caroling helped bring Amy out of her shell. And since the little girl was smiling up at her and singing with her whole heart, Charlotte had no choice but to do the same. From Susan Juettemeyer's round eyes and startled expression, maybe she sang a little too loudly.

But Amy's giggles and spins in response were too precious for her to stop now.

"Wow. Just wow." Tabby was red-faced from laughing.

"We were good!" Amy gushed.

"You were something," Macon said. "You know what your grandpa would say? Give it your all, no matter what you do. Right about now, you're making him proud."

Amy nodded.

"I can sing loud, too." Jilly shrugged out of Macon's arms and ran up, taking Charlotte's other hand. "Let's sing."

"We have to wait until Mrs. Juettemeyer starts a new song." She squeezed their hands. "Let's go to the next house, okay?"

MACON TRAILED BEHIND, watching Charlotte and the twins whisper and giggle. And sing…at the top of their lungs. Susan Juettemeyer wasn't happy about it. Poor woman. Working with her on the decorating committee had taught him how inflexible she was. And, when things didn't go the way she imagined them, she struggled to stay civil. Her pinched smile and narrowed gaze were proof of that. Still, she gritted her teeth and did her best not to wince when Jilly hit an especially high note—high enough to be a threat to Frank Harker's window.

"If you stare much harder, everyone will know you're still crazy about her." Tabby's voice was low.

He glanced at his sister, smiling at one of the shopkeepers who had come out to hear them sing.

"Oh-ho! Not going to deny it anymore." She took his hand, tugging him after the group. "And, so, what does this mean, exactly?"

He shook his head. "Nothing has changed, Tabby. Nothing."

The look on his sister's face said she didn't agree, not in the least. "You're not going to tell her?"

"What?"

"How you feel… That *everything* has changed." Tabby shook her hand free.

As much as he'd like to think it was that easy, he knew better. "I don't think laying it all out there is the right way to go." His quick glance toward Charlotte found her snapping pictures of the girls and the other carolers.

Tabby grinned.

"Stop." He shook his head. "I'm not saying I won't try, okay? But it will be on my terms, without any well-intentioned meddling from my well-intentioned family."

She was still grinning.

He loved his little sister but the gleam in her eyes made him downright nervous. "Tabby..." But his attempt at being stern came out more a plea of desperation. "Come on, now."

"What's that look for?" Charlotte was staring back at them, her gaze widening when she caught sight of Tabby. "Oh-oh. A grin like that means trouble."

Macon nodded. "How right you are."

"Me? Trouble? Nope. Not at all." Tabby winked at the girls. "Looks like we're going to sing for Mr. Harker now, girlies. You ready? Let's get right up by his fence so he can hear you."

Macon shook his head, watching the three of them smile and wave at Frank Harker as he made his way from his porch to midway down the path.

"Seriously," Charlotte whispered to Macon when Tabby and the girls were out of earshot. "That was some face. Whatever she's up to, be afraid."

He didn't want to know. And since it likely had everything to do with his sister doing exactly what he'd told her not to do, he wasn't about to speculate out loud. It was easier to say, "Just Tabby being Tabby."

"Exactly." She smiled up at him. "Meaning she's up to something."

Which was true. But, for now, she was busy with the girls and Charlotte was smiling up at him. He wasn't sure how a smile could stir up so many emotions, but it did. Longing and happiness made his blood thrum. But so was uncertainty—and fear. It had taken him so long to get over her. *Who am I kidding?* He wasn't over her. He never had been.

"Let's sing 'Away in a Manger,'" Susan said, giving those who needed it time to find it in their book of carols. "Ready?"

He heard Jilly's excited, "Ready!" from their spot on the corner. The sheer glee in her voice had him and Charlotte laughing together.

"I think they're having fun." Charlotte was watching Jilly and Amy swing back and forth on Tabby's arms.

But Macon was watching her. *Staring like a fool is more like it.*

"I guess it's hard to get away to Christmas shop when you have two little ones with all that energy underfoot." Charlotte's nose wrinkled. "There can't be much free time to relax."

"Free time is in short supply with those two underfoot." He grinned. "But I can't imagine it any other way."

He only knew the first verse so, when the song started, he flipped to the right page. Charlotte had passed on a book of carols but she leaned close now, her head bent forward to read. Her voice was softer, uncertain, when they got to the third verse he turned, holding the book lower so it was easier for her to see. Then, she lifted her head and sang just as loudly as the girls.

It was sweet and pure and free, her simple joy.

That was something else about Charlotte—she gave her

all, no matter what. He'd always admired that. He still did.

When the song ended, Frank Harker clapped and Pat's tail was wagging. He wasn't sure if it was applause for their performance or thanks that the song was over. Either way, Charlotte was beaming.

"Mr. Harker." Charlotte waved. "Having a nice evening?"

Frank nodded, his lively gaze bouncing between the two of them. "Looking up, I must say."

First Tabby, now Frank Harker.

Luckily, Charlotte was too wrapped up with Pat to notice. "You should come with us." She was leaning over his fence to reach the appreciative German shepherd. "I'm sure Pat would love to stretch her legs. You know, a w-a-l-k? I'm spelling because Fern knows what that word is."

If Macon didn't know better, he'd swear Pat understood anyway. His ears perked up, his tail started wagging.

"Might as well, Frank. We're over the halfway point." Macon nodded. "You don't have to sing. If you stand by Charlotte or the girls, no one will hear you anyway."

Charlotte shot him a look, but her smile never wavered. "Don't listen to him."

Frank seemed to hesitate.

"Please," Charlotte added. "It's too pretty a night not to enjoy it. Where's Pat's leash? I'll get it."

With a resigned sigh, he pointed. "Right inside the door on the hook." But, watching Charlotte sprint up the path and back, breathless and happy, took the starch out of the old man. He was shaking his head as he clipped the leash onto Pat's collar and joined her at his gate. "Maybe for a block or two."

Macon watched the transformation on Frank Harker's face when she hooked her arm through his. Her ability to put people at ease was a gift—not that she saw it. But he did. Macon took Pat's leash and let the two of them wander ahead. Seeing Frank Harker's sudden animation, and the spring in his step, revealed just how fond the man was of Charlotte. *He's not the only one.* While Charlotte was learning all about Frank's day, he let Pat take his time sniffing and exploring—needing space to wrap his mind around the truth his heart was telling him.

"Kittens?" He heard the excitement in Charlotte's voice.

He shook his head. "She always was partial to cats," he told Pat.

Pat didn't seem the least bit interested in this information. He did, however, choose that moment to pick up the pace and catch up to Frank and Charlotte.

"Can't keep up with old Pat?" Frank asked, chuckling. "Who's walking who?"

"Seems like he has someplace to go." Macon shrugged, winking at her as they passed them.

"He likes being the leader," Frank called after them.

Amy, who had a weakness for dogs, deserted the carolers to walk with him and Pat. She pointed out the prettiest Christmas trees or porch decorations until she was yawning and rubbing her little eyes. Then he had no choice. "Gotta get her home, Pat. No more roaming the city streets for you." Pat yawned too, cocked his head, and followed Macon back to Frank. "Looks like Pat and Amy are ready to call it a night."

"Sure." Frank took Pat's leash, chuckling as Amy drooped against Macon's shoulder. "Late night for little ones and us old folk." He lowered his voice. "Might help if you pack those two up with your sister so you can stop dragging your feet and start sweeping her off hers."

"She's right there." Macon nodded at Charlotte, who was chatting with some of the other carolers.

"I know it, boy." Frank Harker nodded. "Don't you let her get away."

Chapter Ten

CHARLOTTE COULDN'T HELP but grin as Amy's voice faded, her head falling forward against Macon's chest before she bolted awake to sing, "Fa-la-la-la-la."

"Not sleepy," Jilly yawned.

"I know," Tabby agreed. "Not one little bit. But your momma and daddy are probably missing you by now." She helped Jilly climb into her car seat. "Plus, I have a secret."

Both girls were wide-eyed when they looked at their aunt.

"Secret?" Jilly whispered.

"What?" Amy leaned forward, away from Macon.

"I *am* tired." Tabby winked.

"Unca Macon bedtime too?" Jilly asked.

"After I make sure Charlotte's home safe and sound." He nodded, walking around the truck to open the rear passenger door. "Let's get you buckled up."

"'Kay," Amy mumbled, her eyelids growing heavy once more.

"Have good dreams." Charlotte waved into the truck. "Christmas and presents and Santa and cookies—"

"Fairies," Amy said, yawning.

"I told you." Macon grinned at her.

"Maybe, if your momma and daddy say it's okay, you

can come have a holiday fairy tea party at my shop tomorrow night?" She paused. "Wings required."

Amy clapped her hands and Jilly squealed.

"I'll take that as a yes?" She was just as excited. The girls were adorable, their energy and laughter contagious in the very best sense. When she'd been little, she'd been just as full of imagination and curiosity. Maybe that's why she wanted to spend more time with them. To rediscover that sense of wonder and delight...

"Great, more wings." Macon's long-suffering sigh made her laugh.

"You look good in wings." Tabby was laughing too. "Besides, only a real man can pull off that look."

Macon rolled his eyes, closed the passenger door, and headed back to the sidewalk where Charlotte stood.

"Who said boys were invited?" she whispered up at him.

"It's because I was teasing you about your singing, isn't it?" he asked.

"Charlotte?" Jilly called, waving her forward.

"Excuse me." Charlotte stepped off the curb and leaned into the truck. "What's up, Jilly?"

"Hugs." She held her arms out. "Night-night hugs."

Charlotte's heart was so full. The feel of the little girl's arms around her neck put a solid lump in her throat. "Night, Jilly. Sleep tight." She couldn't remember the last time someone had vied for her attention—especially someone as precious as Jilly.

"Me too," Amy murmured, her eyes barely open. "Me too."

Charlotte wasn't about to say no. She hurried around to

the other side of the truck and hugged Amy. The brush of the little girl's curls were soft against her cheek. "Sweet dreams Amy."

She closed the truck door and waved through the window before heading back to the sidewalk. First the milkshake, then the caroling, Macon's smile, now the hugs… Today had been one of the best days ever. She didn't want it to end. "I've never had such sweet good-night hugs before." Her voice wavered—she could hear it. And if she heard it—

"You okay?" Macon asked, his blue eyes shining in the glow from the streetlamp overhead. "Charlotte? Are you crying?" The concern in his voice made her eyes burn something fierce.

"No," she sniffed, the lump in her throat bigger. *Possibly.*

He tilted her chin up, his thumb brushing along her cheek, rough but gentle and warm. "You are."

"I…I'm not." She sniffed, wishing she could look away. Away from his blue eyes. Blue eyes that were full of warmth and concern. For her. Intent and unwavering… The longer his gaze held hers, the harder it was for her to breathe. "Maybe." Did she say that out loud?

"Charlotte." It was a whisper, his hand featherlight on her cheek.

Who needed air? Or breathing? Macon was looking at her like… Like he used to look at her. Like she was the only thing that mattered in his world. Like he needed to touch her. And she wanted him to. She ached for him. Warmth and excitement, nerves and anticipation—and panic—had her brain spinning and her heart pounding.

She wasn't sure who stepped closer. It might have been

her. Or Macon. Macon, whose hand slipped around to cradle her head before he stooped—he was a giant after all—close enough to—

"Unca Macon!" Jilly called out. "Hugs! Hugs!"

Her little cry sent Charlotte stepping frantically back—and sliding off the curb.

Macon steadied her, his hands grabbing her shoulders before she slipped and fell. "Good?" He let go as quickly as he'd caught her.

Now he was walking away and she was reeling from...regret? Wait, what? *No...* Not regret. Jilly's giggle jerked her firmly back to reality. One where she and Macon had been inches away—in front of Tabby and the girls and the carolers still ambling along the street to Hildie's. They'd had quite an audience... But none of them had mattered—existed—seconds ago.

"What was *that*?" Tabby whispered, nudging her.

Her heart hadn't recovered enough to answer. Besides, what could she say?

But Tabby wasn't done. She gushed, her voice high and her words rushed. "The looking and the touching and the standing close—"

Yes, she'd been there. For *all* of it.

"Charlotte?" Tabby was wearing that grin again, that 'up-to-no-good' expression.

"You are seeing things." But her words would have been more effective if her voice wasn't breaking.

"Uh-huh." Tabby's grin didn't dim. "Or maybe you're not seeing what's right in front of you?"

That's where Tabby had it wrong. She saw Macon and

the girls and caught a glimpse of how sweet a future for them could be. Her heart was slamming against her ribs, so hard she worried Tabby could hear. Or the carolers. The town. She sucked in a deep breath. "All I see is two very sleepy little girls in your truck." She tried to smile.

"Subtle, Charlotte." But Tabby was laughing again. "Fine. I'll see you later." She hugged her brother. "Night, Unca Macon. You two kids have fun."

"Yeah, yeah." Macon closed the door and waved. He waited until the truck had turned off Main Street to look her way. "Hot chocolate?"

Was that a good idea? More time with him? They'd almost kissed. Hadn't they? In front of…everyone. "Sure." What could go wrong?

"I know, it's a tough call." He walked slowly toward her. "If you have too much sugar, you won't be able to sleep. But you need your sleep because you're decorating for the ball *and* having a holiday fairy tea party tomorrow. And let's not forget Edda Mae's back soon, too." He nodded, pretending to mull it over, rubbing his chin. "*But*, and this is a big but, it's hot chocolate and it's really good—"

She laughed. No matter what the circumstances, Macon always lightened the mood. Like now. Laughing was way better than getting stuck in her head overanalyzing something that hadn't happened. There it was again. The not-so-tiny twinge of regret in the pit of her stomach.

"No?" he asked, the corner of his mouth curving. "Yes?"

"Yes." No more regrets.

"Right answer." He held his hand out.

"There was a wrong answer?" She stared at his hand. No

more regrets. Holding his hand had always felt right. He made her feel safe. Cherished. That hadn't changed. His hand was big and warm around hers. But nothing was as warm as the smile on his face and the spark in his eyes. He was staring, a little too intently and looking a lot too handsome, so she nudged him. "Since when did you become such a big hot chocolate fan?"

"Since I'm having it with you." He squeezed her hand.

Heat flooded her cheeks. He wanted to spend time with her—he'd already said that. But it made her happy to hear him say it again. Very happy. She cleared her throat. "Right answer."

The walk to Hildie's Haus was two blocks but neither of them were in a hurry to get there.

"You rescued kittens?"

"I did." He nodded. "I didn't wear my cape—it might have got me stuck under the porch. But hey, it was still heroic."

She laughed. "Mr. Harker seemed to think so. To hear him tell it, you practically lifted the entire house to get to them."

"Are you saying I didn't?" His blue eyes flashed.

"No. I wouldn't dare suggest such a thing." Her smile wavered, the questions and emotions she'd been fighting welling up before she had time to stop them. "How can you think of leaving, Macon? I mean… This is home—for you. I can't imagine this place, this town, without you being here."

"I could ask you the same thing." His smile dimmed.

"But we're not talking about me." She tugged his hand. "We're talking about you. And this job… You know, the one you should be way more excited about. Is this the job you really want?"

"Who was the one telling me I needed to take more risks? Try new things?" He looked down at her. "To live with no regrets?"

"I was talking about me. Not you. And that was years ago." That he remembered her words was a surprise. "You've built a life here. A wonderful full life. You have a family. Aren't you happy?" Watching him with the twins, Frank, everyone—he had all the love and support a person could ever need. He fit here. She'd never fit anywhere...until now. Still, it wasn't her place to push, no matter how much she wanted to. Instead, she opted for teasing. "Maybe adopting one of Frank's kittens would help. A kitten makes everything better."

They stopped outside of Hildie's Haus. Inside, the lights and music were tempting but Charlotte wasn't going in until she heard his answer to her question.

"A kitten?" He chuckled, shaking his head. "I am happy, but that doesn't mean I won't be happy there. Maybe I'll be even happier. Who knows?" He swallowed. "You remember you told me there was something missing in your life? That there was a hole inside?" He pressed his hand against his chest. "I get it now."

How could she argue with that? She couldn't. Still, hearing him say something was missing hurt. Macon deserved happiness. Real happiness. If something was missing in his life, she wanted him to find it—wherever that took him. But that didn't mean she liked it. While she'd tried not to include Macon on her 'should-she or shouldn't-she buy

Krauss's Blooms and move back here' list, she knew better. He was there, he'd always been there. But now? Her chest ached.

He stared down at their hands, the muscle in his jaw clenching. "You being here? It's more obvious than ever." His gaze met hers, searching. "I don't want to live with this hole anymore, Charlotte..."

"You two coming in?" Susan Juettemeyer had the door wide. "They're almost out of hot chocolate. Besides, it's getting downright chilly."

Charlotte was frozen, his words hanging in the air. He'd had more to say, she knew it.

Macon, however, was nodding at Susan Juettemeyer. "Definitely. Charlotte and I were just talking about the decorations." His hand held hers, guiding her inside Hildie's Haus. In no time, he had a cup of steaming hot chocolate pressed in her hands. "Careful. It's hot." He winked, teasing.

"Imagine that?" But she was smiling.

"Can you believe it? Tomorrow we decorate." Susan nodded. "All the buildup and work and, poof, it's all over in a day. Then all the stress is gone—until we start the planning again in July." She broke off. "I guess I shouldn't brag. You still have the toy drive party, don't you?"

The ball and the party, then Christmas and New Year's. Then what? Macon would leave and she would go where? The shop, her flower café, sprang to mind. It wasn't a surprise—she'd made the place her own. Being back in Last Stand made her happy. There was no place she'd rather be.

MACON STARED AT the pile of chocolate chip pancakes Amy had served him. He'd done his best with the first stack. He'd managed to down the second. But he could feel himself weakening. This wasn't going to be easy.

"Eat up." Amy smiled, a smear of chocolate on her cheek.

Gwen turned from her place at the stove. "Girls, if you keep feeding your uncle pancakes, he'll get a tummy ache. You don't want him to get sick, do you?"

Jilly and Amy stared at his plate, wide-eyed with concern.

He couldn't take it. "I'm still mighty hungry, girls," he assured them, diving into the stack with enthusiasm. "Good stuff."

Jilly nodded.

Amy's gaze remained fixed on his pancakes, looking worried.

"Where are you putting all of that?" Kolton sat opposite him at the large kitchen table, sipping a cup of coffee.

"Hollow leg," Lam suggested, taking a bite of his own pancakes.

"Good morning. Something smells amazing." Tabby walked into the kitchen. "Wow, Macon, I hope you left some for me."

"I get it," Amy offered, trotting across the kitchen to Gwen.

"I help," Jilly added, trailing after her twin.

Macon groaned and sat back in his chair. There was no way he'd be able to finish off this third helping. Once he knew the girls were occupied, he stood up, leaned across the table, then scraped the pancakes onto Kolton's plate.

"Really?" Kolton asked, shaking his head. "You don't want to disappoint them, so I get to do it?"

Lam chuckled from his seat at the head of the table.

"Or you could eat them." Macon sat, stretching his long legs out and cradling his coffee cup between his hands. "What's on today's schedule?"

"Tea party!" Jilly declared, holding one side of the plate that held Tabby's mile-high stack of pancakes.

"Fairy party," Amy added, holding on to the other side of the plate, taking careful steps. "At Char-luttz."

"It was nice of Charlotte to plan this for the girls." Gwen smiled, carrying a platter to the table. "They were so excited last night, I was worried they'd never fall asleep."

"I'm pretty excited, too," Tabby added. "But first, I have to take Charlotte shopping. She was fine letting me buy a dress for her, but I told her she had to go, too. Besides, I know you need me to get her out of the way so you can work your magic."

Macon nodded. Today was going to be nonstop. First, fixing up Krauss's Blooms. Then decorating Jameson House for tomorrow's ball. Then a tea party.

"Magic?" Jilly asked.

Amy's fork paused midway to her mouth. "Unca Macon magic?"

"Close." Gwen took her seat by Lam, kissing his cheek. "He's going to make sure Charlotte's shop looks perfect for the tea party tonight. He's kind of like one of Santa's elves."

Amy's fork dropped to her plate as she clapped.

Jilly squealed.

Lam covered his mouth, and his laughter, with his napkin.

"I don't know. Just the thought of Macon in elf getup?" Kolton asked. "It's not pretty."

Macon ran a hand along the back of his neck. "Really?"

"It will be so much fun." Tabby ignored her brothers, her fork cutting through her pancakes. "Any of you planning on joining us tonight?"

From the smile on Lam and Gwen's faces, Macon suspected the two of them would appreciate some newlywed alone time.

"Kolton?" Tabby asked.

Amy and Jilly's heads swiveled Kolton's way.

"I already made plans." He shrugged. "Besides, I heard wings are required." Kolton had his hands up, his head shaking. "Wearing them here, far from prying eyes, on the ranch is one thing. But in town, with big windows and nosy neighbors with prying eyes? No, sir."

"Macon?" Tabby asked.

Amy and Jilly were staring at him, now, their light brown gazes hopeful.

He hadn't planned on it. But, it was time with Charlotte... "I might." He shrugged. "But, since I'm helping Santa today, how about I wear a Santa hat instead of wings?"

Amy and Jilly faced each other, their faces animated— even though they didn't say a word.

"Okay," Jilly said.

Amy nodded, giving him a thumbs-up.

"Quick thinking." Kolton finished off the pancakes.

"Want some more, Unca Macon?" Jilly asked.

"He looks plenty hungry to me," Kolton offered, trying

not to laugh.

"You two." Gwen sighed. "No more pancakes for your uncles, girls. They have things to do and you need to make Charlotte a thank-you card. You should always thank your host or hostess when they invite you to a party."

"Manners?" Amy asked.

"Yup." Jilly smiled. "Then party."

More squealing and clapping followed.

"I think that's our cue to skedaddle." Kolton stood, carrying his plate to the sink.

Macon followed, rinsing and loading his plate in the dishwasher. "I'll be back for you three in a bit." Which earned him hugs and kisses from his nieces.

While Kolton ticked off the items he still needed to purchase for Christmas, Macon's thoughts drifted to Charlotte. That seemed to be happening more and more these days. He knew their time was running out and, as Frank Harker would say, he needed to up his game. That was why he'd enlisted his brothers' help. He hoped they'd finish up the work at the shop, Charlotte's 'vision board' his guide, before they were due at Jameson House but, if not, Kolt had promised to stay until everything was perfect. When Charlotte walked into the shop tonight, he wanted to take her breath away. He'd always wanted to make her dreams come true, and now he had a chance.

"Hello?" Kolton cleared his throat, loudly, once they were in Macon's pickup. "Earth to Macon?"

He glanced at his brother. "I was listening."

"So, you know what I just said?" Kolton crossed his arms over his chest.

"No."

"Macon, seriously, you're driving me crazy. You have to tell her." He shifted in his seat. "You're driving *everyone* crazy."

"Don't hold back now," Macon sighed, his hands flexing against the steering wheel. "I thought we weren't talking about this."

"I'm not going to not talk about it anymore. You love her. You've always loved her. I know she broke your heart but that was a long time ago. You were only kids back then. Now, you're not. If you want to be with her, be with her. If that means going where she is, go. It's not like you're tied to any place. Not Last Stand. Not Wichita Falls."

Macon stared out the front windshield.

"Are you listening? Because you seem to have a real short attention span right now. From what I can see, you're always thinking about the woman we're not supposed to be talking about." Kolton grinned.

Macon glanced at his brother. "You're right."

Kolton made a big show of bracing himself against the ceiling and the passenger door. "Hold everything. Come again?"

Macon chuckled. "You heard me."

"Oh, I heard you. But I still want to hear it again."

"You. Are. Right." He kept on chuckling.

Kolton sat back against the seat. "I know."

"Don't let it go to your head or anything."

"Too late." Kolton rested his head against the seat. "I'm right. Guess that means you need to make sure your passport is up to date?"

Macon swallowed. "First, I need to find out if she wants me as a traveling companion."

Kolton's groan was pure impatience. "Guess the only way to know is...talk to Charlotte."

He wasn't about to tell his brother he was right, not twice in one day. Kolton already had a healthy self-esteem without him inflating it. After they'd finished at the flower café—making Charlotte's dreams come true, down to the last detail—and tonight's holiday fairy tea party was over, he needed to carve out some time for him and Charlotte. Alone. To talk. To open himself up to all the possibilities.

Even heartbreak.

Chapter Eleven

CHARLOTTE SURVEYED THE transformation of Jameson House. "Silver and gold," she murmured. The grand old house didn't need much really. It was all carved wood, columns, massive windows, and old-world charm. Still the tall, white birch trees strung with twinkling lights formed an elegant entrance. Inside, white-flocked Christmas trees covered with gold and silver balls, bells, snowmen, and more were placed throughout. The dance floor was surrounded by round tables—better for conversation, Susan said—with crisply ironed white tablecloths. Macon insisted that the votive candles in each centerpiece be replaced with the battery-operated sort, but their artificial flicker was just as nice. Charlotte had begged and pleaded, and finally Susan had given in and allowed her to add glitter-dusted pinecones and white flowers to each table, for that extra touch.

She'd taken pictures throughout the day, documenting the hard work of the decorating committee.

Macon zipped back and forth, always ready to lend a hand.

He was up and down ladders—which didn't look very safe to her—to help with last-minute light tweaks, garland adjustments, or any other thing that needed doing.

Her job was to make sure there were no tripping hazards.

She walked around, tape in hand, staring at the floor. Whenever a stray cord or carpet edge looked remotely threatening, Charlotte applied tape. A lot of tape.

"You sure you're using enough?" Macon was standing over her.

She crouched, adding another strip of duct tape over the cord. "If this is my job, I'm going to take it seriously. Rules are rules. They are to be followed—to the letter." She stood. "You can thank the good people on the city historical society for that."

He shook his head, studying her handiwork. "I'll be sure to thank them."

"Did Ned say when the repairs were going to be finished?" She'd been anxious to get back to the shop. Grammy would be home tomorrow and she wanted the place to be perfect—as perfect as possible, anyway.

"Tomorrow morning." He nodded. "What time does Edda Mae get home?"

"Tomorrow afternoon. She's so excited about the ball, I can't really refuse to go, can I?" She followed him across the ballroom, tape in hand.

Macon stooped, opening the legs on one of the eight-foot folding tables lining the periphery of the ballroom. "Go where?"

"To the ball." Not that it wasn't coming together nicely. Seeing the ballroom now, she realized there had been no reason to be skeptical over the whole gold-and-silver theme. Grammy would love it. "It's just not my thing. Still, I don't want to disappoint her, you know?"

Macon stopped working and looked at her. "It's a chance

for her to show you off. She's proud of you, Charlotte."

He said it as if it was the most obvious thing in the world. And, for some reason, it had her flushing with pleasure. Not that it made her any more enthusiastic about going to the Christmas Ball. "I'm pretty sure I've already run into everyone in town." She shrugged. Her original objection had been the lack of a dress, but really, it had been to avoid *talk*. Because she and Macon, together, would create a stir. And since Tabby had talked her into buying a gorgeous red dress, her argument about not having anything to wear was no longer valid. But she still wasn't sure about attending. A dress could be returned—even if she did look amazing in it. Or so Tabby said.

Worrying about gossip wasn't really a good excuse any-more, either. She and Macon had already aroused suspicion with their hand-holding and near kiss after caroling. Every-one in town was talking about them already.

Going to the ball wouldn't be all bad. The fact that she'd have the chance to dance with Macon was at the top of her 'pro' list. She wanted to dance with him, partly because she remembered how well he danced and partly because dancing made it okay to be in his arms. *Which would, again, give people something to talk about.*

"You and Tabby didn't find a dress?" He went back to setting up the tables.

She wrinkled her nose. "We found one." It was breath-taking. When she had it on, she felt beautiful. It was the sort of thing she'd never buy…before. A red evening gown wasn't meant for the living-out-of-a-suitcase lifestyle.

He chuckled. "That bad?"

She shook her head. "It's pretty. Tabby said I look nice. It's just, I don't know, not something I'd normally do."

"Says the woman who was always on me to try things out of my comfort zone." He shrugged. "You have the dress. Edda Mae really wants you there." He ran a hand along the back of his neck. "You should come." He swallowed. "I'll even pick you and Edda Mae up, if you like."

She spun the roll of tape around her arm, staring at the metallic silver material. *If I like?* What would she like? *For him to ask me out on a date.* And that was the last thing she'd expected to pop into her mind. But now that it was there... She blinked, glancing at him. That was only the beginning of her list of wants. Another item? For him to stay in Last Stand. With her. But what she wanted most? *For Macon to be happy.* Which could mean leaving Last Stand. So she needed to keep all her newly formed wants to herself—to avoid complications all around.

He was waiting, his gaze on the roll of duct tape, too.

"Grammy might have a date." She rocked back and forth on the balls of her feet, hoping he wouldn't pick up on her agitation. "Lewis the master gardener," she whispered.

"Yeah, I got that," he whispered back, grinning. "Has she mentioned him? Or said anything about him being on the cruise?"

She shook her head, moving closer. "It's not like her to keep a secret. I'm not sure why."

"Maybe she's worried about what you'll think?" He shrugged, turning over the table and starting to unfold the legs on the next one.

She frowned. "But...why? I mean, why would I be anything but happy for her?" She helped him flip over the table. "If she's happy, I'm happy."

"That simple?" he asked, shaking out one of the table-cloths.

"Why not?" She grabbed the other end of the tablecloth, running her hand across it to smooth the wrinkles. "Happiness is serious business. I wouldn't deprive someone of the chance to be happy."

Macon's brows rose. "Well, then, it would make me happy if you'd come with me to the Christmas Ball tomorrow night."

"Macon Draeger," she gasped. "Are you manipulating me right now?"

"You can call it whatever you want, Charlotte Krauss." His blue eyes sparkled. "What's your answer?"

"Fine. I'll go. I don't want to disappoint Grammy. But you don't have to take me."

"Maybe I want to take you?" he asked.

"Maybe?" she repeated, softly.

"No maybe." He shook his head. "I want to take you, Charlotte."

"Oh." She blinked, struggling not to smile. "Well then." *Give it up.* She grinned. "I want that too." In that instant, she realized she liked the way their gazes locked and tangled up in one another. She had no interest in looking away or bringing this moment to a close. Not when he was looking at her that way. And she was feeling like this.

Blissfully happy.

"What's the matter?" Susan asked. "Is something wrong with the table?" She eyed the table he had half assembled. "Is it broken? I think we might have an extra one in the back."

Macon cleared his throat and tore his gaze away to find Susan looking between them, waiting. "No, no. It's fine. I can make this work." His voice was low and gruff.

"Are you sure?" Susan asked.

"Yes, ma'am." He nodded. "Charlotte and I were just talking about Edda Mae coming home."

Susan nodded, her not-so-subtle glance between the two of them amusing. "I guess that means you'll be off on your next big adventure then, Charlotte?"

"Not yet." Not at all. "Grammy asked me to stay through the New Year."

Susan nodded. "That will make this year's celebration extra special." She patted her arm and walked off, issuing orders to the poor person in charge of setting up the ticket table.

"Through New Year's?" Macon asked, snapping the last leg into place and turning the table over. "Then you're off." It was more of a statement than a question.

"You?" she countered. "When are you leaving? When does the job start?" Maybe Tabby was right. Maybe he wasn't sure about the job. Maybe he hadn't made up his mind yet.

"The job starts January." He looked past her, to the large French doors leading out to the massive wraparound porch outside. "January fifth."

He didn't say 'I'm not sure about the job' or 'I don't know what I'm going to do.' There was no uncertainty at all in his voice. Did that mean he'd made his decision? It looked like it. Macon Draeger was leaving Last Stand. He was leaving and she was staying. And if that was the case, she'd have to make sure she enjoyed every second they had together. "Looks like next year will be all about fresh starts for both of us."

"Come on, come on." Jilly ran down the sidewalk, her extra-sparkly wings bouncing against her back.

Amy was jumping up and down. "Unca Macon."

"I'm coming." He paused outside the large picture window and peered inside. "Let me show you." He scooped them up, one in each arm, and let them get a peek. "What do you think?"

Inside the shop, tiny battery-operated votives flickered on every table, along the counter, and amongst the shelves he and Kolton had assembled earlier. They'd loaded them with the tea, travel books, seed packets, and other bits and bobs Charlotte had begun to stock for sale. Neither he nor Kolt were exactly creative, but he thought they'd done all right.

The eighteen flower pomanders—he knew because Kolton had counted—of various sizes, hung from the lattice secured overhead. The mix of flowers, lights, ribbons and garland, strands of dewdrop crystals and dried clove oranges were...

"Prettiful," Amy whispered. "So, so, prettiful."

"Magic." Jilly was bouncing in his arm. "Let's go."

It was time to see what Charlotte thought. On the drive into town, it occurred to him that he might have overstepped. This was her project, her dream. What if he'd messed it up? Done something wrong?

They pushed through the front door, the cheery little bell ringing.

Christmas carols played softly. On the far table, a fancy silver tea service sat beside a three-tier silver tray that was loaded with tiny sandwiches, tarts, and berries.

"Unca Macon." Amy tugged on his hand.

He stooped. "What's up, Pumpkin Pie?"

Amy's hand gripped his flannel sleeve. Her eyes were wide as she stared all around her.

"Like it?" he whispered. Amy was overwhelmed.

She nodded, her little hand tightening.

Jilly was tiptoeing around the shop, her hands clasped in front of her, moving at a snail's pace.

"You're here." Charlotte came through the workroom door, carrying a gingerbread house. "Look at you. What beautiful fairy princesses you are!"

Macon wasn't sure what was more enchanting—the shop or Charlotte, in fairy wings. "I think they're in shock. I've never seen them so quiet."

But Charlotte was staring at him, a brilliant sheen in her gray eyes. "Macon." She swallowed.

He stood, Amy in his arms.

"I don't even…" She stared around her. "I mean." She blinked. "You did this." Those warm gray eyes searched his face.

"I had some help." He slowly closed the distance between them. "And, I might have taken a long look at your wish list. You're not mad?"

Her brow creased. "Why would I be mad?"

"I don't know? I know how independent you are. I didn't want you to think I doubted your ability...or anything like that." He paused. "To keep you off a ladder as much as possible, I rigged this." He crossed the room, heading toward the wall. "It's a pulley." He showed her the large hook. "You unwind here and the whole lattice lowers. I figured you'll be changing things out with the seasons?"

Charlotte shook her head. "You thought of everything."

He'd wanted to do this for Charlotte but there were practical applications too. "Edda Mae shouldn't be going up and down ladders, either. After you leave—"

"Charlotte." Amy reached for her. "I like your wings."

Charlotte took Amy. "Yours are more sparkly than mine."

"Mine too." Jilly spun.

"Very nice." Charlotte nodded. "Where is Uncle Macon's elf hat? And where is Aunt Tabby?"

"Aunt Tabby is sick," Jilly said. "Her tummy is upsetted."

"Bad." Amy nodded, making a face.

"That bad?" Charlotte looked at him for confirmation.

"That bad." He nodded. "She's not the only one. Gwen and Lam, too. Must be something they ate...I hope." He chuckled.

"Oh." Charlotte's nose wrinkled. "Well, we will just have to have a wonderful time—just the four of us. Are you hungry?" She glanced his way. "Peppermint tea. Decaffeinated."

"That's a relief. Let's get this tea party started."

"Not yet." Charlotte held up one finger and hurried to

the workroom, Amy in her arms. Seconds later, they emerged. "Now we're ready."

Amy held out a red-and-white Santa hat. "For you," Amy chimed. "The party."

"Of course." He cocked an eyebrow at Charlotte but he took the hat. "Now we're ready."

After the tea was gone and the treats were devoured, Charlotte said, "We're going to decorate a gingerbread house. But this isn't just any gingerbread house. This will be a house for fairies."

"It will?" Jilly asked.

Macon stared at Charlotte's gingerbread house. It was lopsided, the irregularly shaped rectangles of gingerbread giving the whole structure a cock-eyed appearance. He saw her nervous glance his way and smiled. "I've never seen a better fairy house."

"Me neiffer," Amy agreed.

"Fairies deserve a special place for the holidays, don't you think?" Charlotte asked. "I have special fairy decorations, too."

Jilly and Amy oohed and aahed over the crystal sprinkles, sugar flowers, pastel-colored gumdrops, and sugar pearls. He did his best to man the frosting—he'd seen Jilly's talent with a tube of frosting firsthand. Besides, the girls had eaten enough sugar.

Charlotte rotated decorating with taking pictures, her delight in the girls warming him through. When the girls laughed, she laughed. When Jilly plopped a blob of frosting on the side of the house, Charlotte carefully—with the help of a lollipop stick, the tip of her tongue sticking out from her lips as she concentrated—managed to spread it without moving anything else. He snatched up her camera then, taking a few pictures, himself.

It was when they were cleaning up that Amy started to droop.

"You okay, Amy?" he asked.

She shook her head. "Tummy."

He and Charlotte exchanged a look.

"Bad," Amy added, pressing both hands against her stomach.

He stared at the mess on the table. "Charlotte—"

"Macon." She shook her head. "Take her home. Poor thing. I hope it's not all the sugar."

He shook his head. "If everyone at home wasn't under the weather, I might agree. But, they are, so I'm thinking whatever they have, it's spreading."

Charlotte's nose wrinkled. "Have a hazmat suit handy?"

She had a point. The last thing he wanted was to get sick. He didn't have time for that—to miss out on spending time with her. "I might just bunk at the firehouse." He chuckled. "But first, I'll get these fairies home and into bed."

"Thank you," Jilly said, yawning.

"You are welcome." Charlotte hugged her close. "I've never had a better holiday fairy tea party before. Ever." Then she whispered, "Not that I've ever thrown one before."

"This was good. If I thought like Tabby, I'd say this was another possible income stream for the shop. Tea parties. Fairy tea parties." He shrugged. "But I'm not Tabby. And I probably have no idea what I'm talking about."

Charlotte was staring at him.

"Charlotte? Forget I mentioned it." He nodded. "We'll get out of your way."

She blinked, several times, then shook her head. "I'll help."

There was a nip in the air so Macon moved quickly. He got the girls buckled into their car seats and covered them up with their snuggly blankets before he turned to Charlotte.

He wasn't prepared for the hug. Charlotte. His Charlotte. Her arms wound around his neck, holding on tight. Her head rested against his chest, her hair brushing against his chin—silky soft. Out of instinct, he buried his nose in her hair. The air was knocked from his lungs and, for a second, he froze. But the moment he realized what was happening, his arms were already around her.

"Thank you, Macon," she whispered. "Thank you, for everything." She stared up at him, looking just as rattled as he was. "Good night." She stepped back, letting him go.

He'd never felt so cold. "Charlotte."

"Amy's sick." She shook her head. "There are some things we need to talk about, I know that. But I'll see you tomorrow. You're my...date, right?"

He grinned. "I am your date."

"Right." She took a few steps backward. "Until tomorrow."

He nodded, climbing into the truck and heading home, knowing he wasn't going to get much sleep tonight.

Chapter Twelve

"CHARLOTTE, THIS IS…" Grammy stared around the shop. "You did this?"

"With some help." Macon. Sweet Macon. She didn't remember writing down all the tiny details but, somehow, he'd managed to know just what she'd envisioned. And this, all of it, was better than her imagination. He'd done this for her. Knowing that, seeing this, filled her heart with hope.

"And these." Grammy studied her latest batch of pictures that had been spread across the counter. At first glance, they might seem unremarkable—a glimpse into an everyday world. But every moment had been a treasure for her. Walks with Fern. Frank Harker and Pat. The carolers, singing in festive sweaters. The twins making monster cookies. Macon, holding Amy—wearing a Santa hat. The large Christmas tree outside the library, shining with multicolored lights. She'd get some of them framed and hung, but others were just for her. "This is home. My little town, all colorful and lively and full of family. There's love here, Charlotte. Love for this place and these people." Her grammy's gaze met hers.

"There is." She blew out a deep breath. "I may not have lived here my whole life, but I do think of Last Stand as my home."

Grammy's eyes crinkled from the width of her smile. "I

know you do." She moved more pictures around, then looked up at the canopy overhead. "Who'd have thought of such a thing?" She shook her head. "You would, of course. You have such a gift, Charlotte." Her gaze sparkled with pride. She patted the photos. "So many gifts."

"Thanks, Grammy." One of her favorites pictures, of the girls caroling—at the top of their lungs if she remembered correctly—lay on top of the stack. Macon was there, too, staring down at the girls with a broad grin creasing his handsome face.

"Plenty of Macon in here." Grammy lifted another photo, one of just Macon.

"Well, thanks to you, I've spent quite a bit of time with him." The picture showed Macon surveying the Jameson House, his hands on his hips and his eyes fixed on some spot across the room. He'd looked so...capable. And handsome. Handsome enough to have her flushing now, just looking at the image. *Macon. What am I going to do about you?* It was a question she'd been pondering for the last couple of days. And since she still hadn't come up with an answer that felt right, she might as well try to enjoy her grammy instead. She set the picture aside and carried their tea to one of the café tables.

"From that smile, I'd say the shop isn't the only thing that's been getting some TLC?" Grammy sat and sipped on the oolong tea Charlotte had made for her. "Happy to hear all my shameless matchmaking paid off."

"Grammy." She almost choked on her tea. She'd suspected as much, but to hear her grandmother admit it outright was something else. From the looks of it, Grammy wasn't the least bit apologetic. If anything, she seemed proud of herself. "Did you know he's moving?"

"Macon?" Her shock said it all. "Macon Draeger? That boy can't leave."

"Well, he seems to disagree." She stood, straightening the shelves and fiddling with the postcards tacked to the wall. "He got some new job offer, though I'm not sure that he wants it. If he wanted it, he'd be excited. Only he's not. I've tried to talk to him about it but he keeps changing the subject. It's like he doesn't want to talk about it with me."

"Why would he?" Grammy took a sip. "You were the one who broke his heart, as I recall. And I have a theory."

Charlotte frowned. She didn't want to hear what Grammy was thinking. And she really didn't like hearing that she'd broken Macon's heart. Yes, she'd been the one to officially end their relationship. But her heart had been broken, too.

"I don't think that boy has ever gotten over you." Grammy was watching her. "The last nine years, he's been waiting for you to come home."

Charlotte stopped pacing. "Waiting?" Why? If that was true, then why was he leaving now that she was here? Not that he knew this was going to be her permanent home—she'd yet to share that with anyone. If he knew, would he stay? If he knew and still didn't stay, would her poor heart ever recover? No, Grammy had to be wrong. She was, after all, holding out for some sort of happy ending between the two of them. That's what she wanted and she tended to get what she wanted.

It's what I want too, Grammy.

Grammy looked at the large round clock on the wall. "We need to head home if we're going to make it on time." She stood. "There's someone I'd like you to meet."

"Lewis?" She carried the empty teacup to the sink and washed it. "Did he enjoy the cruise?" It took a lot to surprise Grammy, but she'd managed it. "I thought I'd check up on him, just to make sure he was the right sort of fellow to be dating my grandmother. I guess you think so..." She waited, watching her grandmother's reaction as she dried the teacups.

Grammy recovered well. "He surprised me. I was walking on the deck and there he was. With flowers, of course. And, Charlotte, we had so much fun. He's quite the traveling companion." Grammy's gaze met hers, her smile hesitant. Macon was right. It looked like Grammy was worried she'd disapprove. It was the first time her grammy had ever seemed nervous.

"I'm so happy for you, Grammy." Charlotte hurried to her side and hugged her tight, eager to reassure her. "I mean it. I can't wait to meet him. But I know if you love him, I will love him, too."

"Well, no one said a thing about love..." Her grammy was blushing.

Blushing. Grammy was blushing. *This is serious.*

While Charlotte locked up the shop, Grammy clipped Fern's leash on. They chatted all the way back to the cottage, catching up on Grammy's adventures, her favorite stops on the cruise, and talking a bit more about Lewis the master gardener, aka: Grammy's boyfriend.

Grammy was happy. It was up to Charlotte to follow her

lead. "Grammy." She paused outside the gate, the gate Macon had fixed, and took her grandmother's hand. "I want to buy Krauss's Blooms. I want to run Krauss's Flower Café. And I want to live here—to come home."

"You do?" Edda Mae was wide-eyed. "Are you sure, Charlotte?"

"I am." She shrugged. "But I don't plan to retire my suitcase completely. I'm going to hire someone to help out in the shop so I can do some freelance work, once or twice a year. Other than that, I want to buy some nonessential clothes, maybe some impractical shoes, makeup, settle down…and be happy. Being here, working in the little shop, spending time with my friends…it makes me happy."

"It's a good plan, Charlotte." Edda Mae grinned. "I confess, that's what I wanted. Thinking of the shop in someone else's hands just about made me sick to my stomach. You've always blossomed there, just like a flower. I'm so glad you'll be taking care of it. No one could do it better." They walked down the path, arm in arm. "You hear that, Fern? Charlotte's going to stay put."

Fern's little tail wagged.

"She approves." Grammy laughed, closing the front door behind them and removing Fern's leash. "What does Macon have to say? Maybe that's why he's not excited about this new job? You're here. And now he's not going to be."

"I haven't told him. I haven't told anyone but you, Grammy." She saw Grammy's scowl. "What is that look for?"

"Charlotte Louise Krauss, you must tell him. That boy can't make a life-altering decision without knowing all the facts."

"Grammy, it's not going to matter. My being here won't affect anything." She paused. "And, just to clear things up, he is not the reason I'm staying."

"He might not be the only reason, but he's one of them," Grammy argued. "And if it won't matter to him, there's no reason not to tell him, is there?"

Charlotte didn't answer. No, according to her logic, telling him wouldn't make a difference to him—one way or the other.

"Is there?" Grammy repeated.

"I guess not." Except she was afraid. There was no denying something was between them. She saw it in his eyes, felt it when he took her hand... *But.* Reminiscing over the past, flirting, and enjoying one another's company didn't translate into a relationship. There was absolutely no guarantee he felt as strongly as she did. That he loved her like she loved him.

Because she did. She loved him. With her whole heart.

"Lewis is meeting me at the ball. I can't wait for you to meet him." Her grandmother was smiling like a schoolgirl with a crush. "And he will be happy, too—to know you're buying the shop, that is. He knew that's what I wanted—I'd told him as much. He's already talking about us taking more adventures together."

Charlotte laughed. "Well, I fully expect a postcard from every port of call."

"You better believe it." Grammy laughed, too, taking Charlotte's hand and leading her down the path to the cottage. "Now, then, let's get all fancied up and go dazzle the menfolk of this town. I hope you can drive in heels, because

I can't."

"Oh, well, Macon was coming to pick us up." Why that made her nervous, she didn't know. But she was. Nervous. Excited. Hopeful. Uncertain. Not about how she felt or what she wanted, but whether or not to share how she felt and what she wanted. With Macon.

"Good." Grammy nodded. "Good. Can't wait to see him. I'm off to get dressed. Are you wearing that pretty pink dress you wore to homecoming?"

"No, Grammy, I'm not. Tabby and I went shopping. I think this dress might be a bit better than the pink one." At least, she hoped so.

"I'm glad to hear it, Charlotte." She patted her cheek. "I know you weren't excited about tonight but—"

"I wasn't Grammy, you're right. But I think, I hope, to-night will be special." Or it would be, if she was brave enough to tell Macon what was in her heart. "We'll see." She pressed a kiss against her cheek. "After all, I get to meet your boyfriend."

MACON PACED BACK and forth on the front porch of Edda Mae Draeger's pink cottage. He hadn't had a case of nerves this bad since...well, the last time he'd been about to tell Charlotte he loved her. They'd been in high school then, a long time ago. Somehow, all the time they'd spent apart had melted away and he was right back where he'd been. Hearth thumping, palms sweating, out of breath, and pacing until he pulled it together.

And he had to pull it together. This wasn't high school. This was here and now. And he had to think of his future. A future with Charlotte or one on his own. Either way, he'd make it work, move on, do his best. But only one would truly make him happy. And the thought of losing that, losing her, put a lump in his throat and a chill down his spine.

"Macon?" Charlotte's voice startled him.

He spun and froze. Charlotte was a vision. Her dark hair was swept up, her long graceful neck exposed. The ruby-red dress set matched the color on her lips—and the color flooding her cheeks. "You look incredible." The words didn't do her justice. She looked... "Beautiful." He swallowed, that lump sticking.

"You look pretty good yourself, cowboy." She smiled, giving him a head-to-toe appraisal. "Nice boots."

"I can't say I'm a fan of a coat and tie, but it's the proper thing to do. Still, you can't expect me to trade in my boots for dress shoes—that would be taking things too far." He loved the little shake of her head as she laughed. "No one is going to be looking at me tonight, I guarantee it."

Her breath caught; he heard it. So he stepped closer.

"I agree." Edda Mae Krauss leaned out the door. "Now, if you two are ready, let's get this show on the road. I have a sweetie waiting for me."

He chuckled, accepting the older woman's hug. "Good to have you back, Edda Mae."

She patted his cheek. "Good to be back." She turned and locked the door. "For now."

"Let me guess? You've been bitten by the travel bug?" He nodded, glancing Charlotte's way. "I hear it's impossible to shake." Still, if Charlotte would have him, he'd follow her wherever she went.

"I'm not so sure about that." Edda Mae winked at Charlotte. "You ready?"

Macon was content to let Edda Mae chatter the whole ride to Jameson House. If she filled the silence, he didn't have to talk. Instead, he tried to come up with just the right thing to say to Charlotte. No matter how hard he tried, nothing sounded right. Now, with her beside him, it took everything he had not to blurt it all out. Tonight would be a challenge. There was nothing like putting your heart out there to make you humble. But Charlotte was worth it.

He parked the truck and escorted them, one on each arm, up the stairs and inside the grand old house.

"Look at that." Edda Mae nodded in approval as she surveyed the ballroom décor. "That Susan runs a tight ship, but she always pulls it together."

"That she does." On both counts.

"You two have some fun. I'm off to find Lewis." Edda Mae waved. "We'll track you down later."

Macon risked another look at Charlotte—and was knocked for a loop all over again. She was breathtaking. While she was smiling and waving at folk across the room, he was staring at her, wondering how he'd ever let her go to begin with.

She caught him watching her. "What? Do I have lipstick on my teeth? I don't normally wear it."

He shook his head, trying not to spend too long studying her mouth. "No lipstick."

"Oh. No?" Her eyes sparkled. "Well, you're sort of staring."

"I know." He shook his head. "I can't take my eyes off of you."

Her breath hitched. "You're full of compliments to-night."

"Am I?" He blew out a deep breath. "Guess I should have been giving you more all along."

It was her turn to stare. Maybe he had a chance after all? Maybe her blushes and smiles could mean he still had a place in her heart? *Don't get ahead of yourself.*

"Macon. Charlotte," Susan Juettemeyer called to them. "We're taking a committee picture." She waved them forward.

"Let's do this." Macon offered her his arm. "Duty calls."

She took his arm, laughing. "Speaking of duty, I plan on focusing solely on safety infractions tonight, just so you know. I might even have to borrow your clipboard."

"Sounds serious."

"Oh, believe me, it is. I might even have duct tape in my purse," she whispered.

"It fit?" he asked, holding up her sequin-covered clutch.

"Barely. I think I might have ripped a seam." She shrugged. "But I managed to get a lipstick in there, too."

"All those years of living out of a suitcase paid off." He covered her hand with his. "Hopefully you can squeeze in a dance or two with me at some point?"

"I'll consider it." But there it was again, that look—the one that caught and held and flooded his chest with pleasure.

"Let's go, let's go." Susan was getting impatient. "Don't you two make a fine couple?"

"I need everyone to squeeze in," the photographer said. "Close."

"Well, all right, then." Charlotte grinned as the group moved closer, squishing her against his side. "Sorry." The back of her hand pressed against his, their fingers brushing.

That was all it took to have his head start spinning, again. And, when her fingers threaded with his and gave his hand a squeeze, his heart rate kicked up a few notches.

"One more," the photographer called out. "Smile… Got it."

"Charlotte, I just wanted to thank you." Susan Juette-meyer was in a very good mood, tonight. Either she'd had some wassail or she was just relieved to have the stress of putting this together over with. Either way, it was a nice change. "I know this town doesn't have the flash and excitement you're used to but, if you ever come back—or decide to stay put—I'd love to have you on board again." She almost smiled. "You two enjoy your night."

"You should feel flattered," Macon said, once Susan and the decorating committee had dispersed. "She doesn't hand out praise lightly."

Charlotte stared after the woman, looking thoughtful.

"As was evidenced by her complete lack of acknowledgment for all of my hard work," he added.

Charlotte laughed. "We did a good job. *You* did an *amazing* job." She hugged his arm. "Can I be honest?"

Her conspiratorial tone had him leaning in. "I'd prefer that."

"I wasn't so sure about the silver and gold theme." Her whisper wasn't really a whisper.

"I'm sorry, was that supposed to be some sort of secret?" His brow dropped. "Because you're squeaking sort of tipped me off back at our first meeting."

"I guess subtlety has never been one of my strong points." She smiled.

"You said it, not me." The fact that he could read every thought on her face had always been a comfort. It was only toward the end that she'd learned to mask her true emotions. He'd hated that—losing that connection. He wanted it back. Wanted her back.

"Hey." She pushed against his shoulder.

"Don't look now, but I see your grandmother." He paused. "I bet the man she is talking to is Lewis."

"The boyfriend." She nodded. "She told me about him. I had to poke a little, but she finally spilled the beans. He surprised her on the cruise. But, considering she was blushing and smiling, it seems to have gone well." She paused. "My grandmother blushed. I couldn't believe it."

He chuckled. "But you're happy?"

She looked up at him. "I'm happy."

"Dance with me?" His brows rose. "If I spin you just right, we can spy on them."

"Oh, well, if that's the reason. I mean, I guess that sort of ties into the whole safety thing? Keeping my grammy's heart safe?" Her nose wrinkled—it was a tic of hers, one he'd always found adorable and all-Charlotte. "That's sort of a stretch."

"I'm good with it." He led her onto the dance floor. "For Grammy."

She was laughing when he put his arm around her and

drew her closer. Then her laughter died down and she was looking up at him. If only he could read her thoughts the way he used to. Still, Charlotte Krauss was back in his arms. Right where she belonged. Now all he had to do was convince her of that.

Just when they were beginning to relax, the music stopped and Susan Juettemeyer tapped the microphone on the small stage.

"Welcome to Last Stand's Annual Christmas Charity Ball. We have a few bits of business to discuss." She rattled off the amount of money they'd raised for scholarships so far, thanked the sponsors, and reminded everyone that they would be needing volunteers for the Fourth of July festivities. "A final bit of business. One of our committee members is stepping aside, so we will have an opening on the decorating committee. It is a volunteer position but, without it, we would not be able to organize amazing events like this one. If there is anyone interested, please let me know and we'll proceed with a confirmation. Edda Mae, thank you for your years of service—"

"It's been my pleasure." Edda Mae stepped up to the microphone—leaving Susan more than a little flustered. "I want to put my two cents in here about this opening. It will take the right person, someone with creativity and a spark, someone who thinks outside the box and shakes things up a bit."

Macon heard Charlotte's soft groan, felt her hand tighten around his. But he didn't know why.

"That's why I'd like to suggest my granddaughter, Charlotte Krauss. Now that she's the owner of Krauss's Blooms—

correction: Krauss's Flower Café, I'm sure she'd love to take my spot on the committee. She has big plans for the shop and a big heart to match."

Edda Mae's little speech earned applause from the room, but Macon was too stunned to join in.

"You're staying?" His voice shook. Charlotte was staying. The thump of his heart was so loud, he couldn't hear the murmurings of the people around him.

All he saw and heard was Charlotte, looking up at him and saying, "I'm staying."

It didn't matter that all eyes were on them or that they were holding hands for all to see. Nope. What mattered was Charlotte. Her sweet smile. And how much he loved her.

Chapter Thirteen

CHARLOTTE WANTED TO ignore her grandmother's request, but since she'd said, "Come on up here, Charlotte," into the microphone, that was sort of hard to do. There were things she had to say. Not to the good people of Last Stand, but to Macon. From the look on his face, he had plenty to say, too. Things she needed to hear.

Macon's hand squeezed hers, then let it go. "That sounded like an order to me." His eyes swept over her face.

"It's just..." She needed to talk to him, alone. But the entire population of the ballroom was avidly watching them so she nodded. "I'll be back."

"I'll be right here." The corner of his mouth curled. And his eyes, oh so blue, never wavered from her face.

How she managed to cross the room and climb the steps onto the portable stage was a mystery. Her legs were shaking. Not because her grandmother was putting her in front of a crowd but because she had no idea what Macon was thinking about her plans.

"We don't have to do this now," Susan was saying.

"Might as well, we're all here." Grammy was smiling. "Anyone else interested?"

No one moved. Macon had mentioned how difficult it was to find people to serve on the committee. Susan had a reputation for getting things done, yes. But that wasn't all. Word of her impatience, perfectionism, and occasional snide comments had gotten out, making already scarce volunteers even scarcer.

By the time Charlotte reached the podium, she was doing her best to smile. She mouthed 'sorry' to Susan and stood by her grammy.

"Well, all right then," Susan's voice was razor sharp, her smile pained. "As Edda Mae, said, we might as well do this now."

There was laughter from the crowd.

"We're so very glad you're staying, Charlotte." Susan was surprisingly sincere. "I have enjoyed working with you this year and would be delighted to do so again next year. If that's what you'd like, we'd love to have you."

"Of course, she does," Grammy offered up.

"Charlotte?" Susan pointedly ignored her grandmother's declaration.

"I'd love to." She nodded. Why not? If Macon stayed, they'd be working together. If he went…she'd have something to keep her from missing him through the holidays. "Thank you."

"Do I have a motion?" Susan called out to the crowd.

She was voted in unanimously. Once she'd read over the policies and procedure manual Susan promised to get her, she'd know exactly what she'd just been signed up for.

But, for now, she needed to get back to Macon. She helped Grammy down the steps from the stage, peering through the crowd for some sign of him. Considering his giant status, he should be easy to find.

"Charlotte, I want you to meet Lewis." Grammy was leading her to the far side of the ballroom.

Lewis. "Of course." Macon would understand. And she could be patient for a few minutes longer. Hopefully. "I'm not sure Susan appreciated how you handled that, Grammy. I'm not sure I did, either."

Grammy smiled over her shoulder. "I had to make sure Macon had all the information—in case you were thinking about not telling him."

"Grammy." There was no point chastising her. Grammy was Grammy. "I can't believe you."

"You'll thank me for it," she said, without an ounce of remorse. "You will."

"I hope you're right." Charlotte sighed. *About everything.*

"Stop worrying for now." She tugged her between two of the round tables to one in the back corner.

Lewis Greer was on his feet before they'd reached the table. He was bald, with a close-trimmed white beard and mustache and metal-rimmed spectacles. And he was short, no taller than Grammy. But the smile he had for her grandmother instantly won Charlotte over. And he wasn't alone in what he was feeling. Grammy took one look at him and lit up.

"Charlotte, dear, this is Lewis Greer." She hooked arms with him. "Lewis, this is my precious granddaughter."

"I have heard so much about you." Lewis held his hand out. "It's a delight, Charlotte, a real delight."

"You too, Mr. Greer." She shook his hand.

"Lewis, please." He continued shaking her hand. "And I want you to know, Edda Mae had no idea I was going to surprise her on that cruise. She's worried you'll think she's keeping secrets from her."

"Which I would never do." Grammy took her hand. "You know that."

Charlotte smiled. "Thank you, Lewis. I do value the honesty and trust I have with my grammy. She is pretty important to me."

Lewis cleared his throat. "To me, as well."

Grammy's look of pure adoration melted away whatever reservations Charlotte had about the two of them.

"Will you join us?" Lewis asked.

"Oh, no, she can't." Grammy shook her head. "She's got to go find Macon and come to some sort of understanding."

"Macon? Her fella?" Lewis asked.

"Well, that's what we're hoping for anyway." Grammy nodded. "But you know young people. They don't seem to be in a hurry to do anything."

Lewis's gaze narrowed as he peered over the rim of his glasses, staring just over her shoulder. "I'm guessing that tall fellow over there is Macon?"

"The one staring at Charlotte?" Grammy chuckled. "That's him all right. Looks like you'll get to meet him, since he's headed this way. Charlotte, breathe. It's all going to work out."

She took a deep breath and turned.

Macon Draeger had paused to check his phone, a furrow creasing his forehead before he tucked it back into his pocket. With a few long strides, he was standing at her side, stealing her breath all over again.

"Edda Mae. Lewis, good to see you again." He held his

hand out. "Been a few years."

"It has. Surprised you remember." Lewis shook his hand. "That was a nasty turn of oak wilt."

"It was. Nature likes to keep things interesting." He glanced back and forth between her grandmother and Lewis. "Speaking of interesting, I hear the two of you went on a cruise?"

Charlotte elbowed him in the side.

But Grammy and Lewis just laughed.

"Lewis likes surprises." Grammy shrugged. "It was a lovely one."

Lewis shot her grandmother another sweet smile.

"Surprises can be a good thing." Macon was staring at her, the weight of his gaze pressed against her chest. "I had one tonight myself."

She glanced up at him. "A good surprise?"

"I think so. Not sure yet." His gaze was searching. "I have to go."

That was the last thing she'd expected him to say. "You're leaving?" Even she heard the disappointment in her voice.

"Got a call." There was the smallest smile on his face.

"Oh, right." Her forehead furrowed. "Be careful." She stepped forward. "Please."

He was full-on smiling then. "Safety is my thing, Charlotte. You don't need to worry." He winked. "Lewis, can I count on you to give the ladies a ride home?"

"It would be my pleasure," Lewis said. "Good seeing you again, Macon."

"You too. Enjoy your night." Macon walked across the

ballroom toward the door.

Charlotte almost looked away, almost. But she was so glad she didn't. If she had, she'd have missed one of his blinding smiles and a wink—just for her.

MACON STARED INTO the gift box at his side. He'd done the wrapping himself, so there was a lot of tape and patched Christmas wrapping paper, but the inhabitant of the box didn't seem to mind. The little kitten stared up at him, purring.

"For something so little, you sure do make a lot of noise." He chuckled. "Guess that means you're happy."

He pulled up in time to see Lewis and Edda Mae, Fern in tow, heading down the street. They waved, smiled, and kept right on walking.

"Think they know something is up?" The kitten didn't answer—he was too busy purring and kneading the fleece blanket Mr. Harker had lined the box with. "I'm going to put this lid on, now, but it won't be on for long." There were holes all along the sides of the box, but Macon still hurried down the path once the lid was on.

The purring continued so Macon figured the little guy was okay for now.

He walked to the cottage and paused, staring at the wreath on Edda Mae's front door. Now that he was here, his stomach was in knots. Since he'd woken up this morning, he'd had one goal—to keep Charlotte in his life. If last night meant what he hoped it meant, he'd have everything he'd ever wanted—Charlotte. Here. And, if he was lucky, there'd be a future for them. If not, well, he'd survive. She'd always have his heart. Then again, she always had.

He blew out a deep breath and knocked.

She opened the door and blinked, her eyes going wide when she saw him. "It's seven in the morning."

And she was wearing a red, white, and green plaid flannel nightgown. "Good morning to you too. You match your Christmas wreath." He grinned, shifting the box.

"It's...seven." She glanced down at her nightgown. "Macon—"

"I brought your present." He waited, smiling when her gaze met his. "I know it's early but can I come in?"

"Yes." She stepped back, a mix of uncertainty and concern creasing her forehead. "It's not Christmas yet. Or, are you not planning on staying through Christmas?"

"I didn't want to wait." He followed her into the living room, spotting the small Christmas tree decorated with ornaments Charlotte had made years ago. "I remember some of these." He turned, shaking his head at the extent of the decorations. "You and Edda Mae went all out, didn't you?" Garland was draped across the fireplace and stockings—one for Edda Mae, one for Charlotte, and one for each of Charlotte's parents—hung from shiny silver hooks. There was a smaller one, for Fern, hanging at the end. Other decorations covered every available surface: Christmas tree and snowman candles, nutcrackers of various sizes, and a tiny village set up on glitter cotton batting.

She nodded. "We're not quite done." Her eyes fixed on the tree. "You know how it is with us. Christmas is a big deal."

"I do. And now you have a Christmas present. Are you going to open it?" he asked, holding out the box.

"Now?" She took it, still not meeting his gaze.

"Yes. The sooner the better." He crossed his arms over his chest. "Careful. It's breakable."

She sat on the couch and cradled the box on her lap. In the silence, it was impossible to miss the noise coming from inside. Charlotte bent closer, her ear pressed against the paper. Her head popped up and her gray eyes locked with his. "You didn't?" But she was already tugging off the lid. "You did."

The kitten chose that moment to meow.

Charlotte lifted him out and held him close, their noses inches apart. "You are the sweetest little thing I have ever seen." The purring intensified. "So tiny." She held the ball of fluff against her chest. "Macon, you didn't have to."

"You said everything was better with a kitten." He shrugged. "He's gray, like your eyes. And, since I had something important I need to tell you, I figured the kitten could only help."

She was staring at him, her smile dipping. "You're taking the job?"

She didn't want him to go. It was easier to breathe, then. The uncertainty pressing against his chest with a vice-like grip melted away. And the rhythm of his heart grew steady once more. Because she didn't want him to go. And all the words he wanted to say clogged up his throat. Instead, he said, "I was hoping you'd go to the Christmas toy drive party with me? Pass out your cookies? Help with the kids?"

Her brow furrowed. "You're here to ask me to…to the toy drive party?"

He sighed, shook his head, and stared at the large advent calendar hanging on the wall. Counting down the days to Christmas. *No more wasting days. No more.* "No. I mean, yes. I came here to say you were right, Charlotte." He stood, pacing to the tree and back. "About the job. I wasn't excited about it. I wanted to be, I really did. I was looking for something, hoping. But, deep down, I knew that job couldn't fill the hole in my heart." He stopped, close enough to reach for her. "Only one thing will do that. And that's you."

"Me?" she repeated, her frown giving way to confusion.

"You. So, yes, I am asking you to go to the toy drive party. And everything else, too. I know you're staying here doesn't mean you want to try again—for us to try again—"

"Macon, that's not true." She shook her head, standing, the kitten cradled against her chest. "I'm staying here no matter what you decide about this job. This is my home. That's my shop. And these are my friends…my family. But what I want, more than anything, is to share it with you." She reached out, resting one hand against his chest.

Macon smiled, blowing out a long slow breath. "I was hoping you'd say that." He stepped forward, his hands cradling her face. "I wanted to tell you the other night, but Tabby got sick too, and there was no one still standing to watch over Amy."

"You're a good uncle and an amazing brother. You take care of people, keep them safe." She smiled. "That's why you're the one I want to put down roots with, Macon."

"They're already there. Deep and strong and solid." He rested his forehead against hers. "I've loved you since I was fifteen years old and nothing will ever change that."

"No matter where I was in the world, my heart was always was always here with you." She slid her hand up to rest on the back of his neck. "Where it belongs."

He nodded, bending to press his lips to hers. Kissing Charlotte was everything he remembered. Soft and warm, a tender promise of a love that would endure. He felt whole and strong and full of hope as he breathed her in and held her close. The sort of happiness welling inside was the only gift Charlotte Krauss ever needed to give him.

"I'm hoping this means you're staying?" she whispered.

He lifted his head, content just to look at her. "As soon as I heard you'd bought the shop, I knew I couldn't leave. Besides, who else are you going to call when you need repairs?" He paused. "Especially if that fire marshal keeps handing out fines. I'm staying."

"I'll take the fines and the repairs." She grinned. "Either way, I get you. I love you, Macon."

"I love you." He ran his thumb along her cheek. "Not that I'm arguing with you..." His gaze searched hers. "Because this is everything I want, right here. But are you sure about giving up on your job?" He cleared his throat. "I don't want you to have any regrets—"

"There's nothing to regret, Macon." She shook her head, pressing her fingers against his lips. "I'm not as selfless as you think. I've been offered a contract position with a magazine. Once or twice a year, I'll go who knows where. And, maybe—hopefully, if you're interested, you could come with me.

If you want to. But you don't have to—"

"I want to." He grinned.

"Good. I'm glad. I've lost too much time with you already." She tightened her arm around his neck and pulled him back for another kiss.

"We'll have a lot to make up for," he whispered against her lips. "Starting now."

The End

If you enjoyed this book, please leave a review at your favorite online retailer! Even if it's just a sentence or two it makes all the difference.

Thanks for reading *Christmas Flowers* by Sasha Summers!

Discover your next romance at TulePublishing.com.

TULE
PUBLISHING

If you enjoyed *Christmas Flowers,*
you'll love the next book in….

The Draegers of Last Stand, Texas series

Book 1: *Sweet on the Cowboy*

Book 2: *Christmas Flowers*

Book 3: *Coming April 2020!*

Available now at your favorite online retailer!

If you enjoyed *Christmas Flowers*, you'll love these other Last Stand, Texas Christmas books!

Christmas for the Deputy
by Nicole Helm

Under the Mistletoe
by Eve Gaddy

A Lone Star Christmas
by Justine Davis

Available now at your favorite online retailer!

About the Author

Sasha Summers grew up surrounded by books. Her passions have always been storytelling, romance and travel—passions she's used to write more than 20 romance novels and novellas. Now a best-selling and award winning-author, Sasha continues to fall a little in love with each hero she writes.

From easy-on-the-eyes cowboy, sexy alpha-male werewolves, to heroes of truly mythic proportions, she believes that everyone should have their happy ending—in fiction and real life.

Sasha lives in the suburbs of the Texas Hill country with her amazing and supportive family and her beloved grumpy cat, Gerard, The Feline Overlord. She looks forward to hearing from fans and hopes you'll visit her online at sashasummers.com.

Thank you for reading

Christmas Flowers

If you enjoyed this book, you can find more from all our
great authors at TulePublishing.com, or from your favorite
online retailer.

Printed in Great Britain
by Amazon